DIARY OF THE DISPLACED

BOOK 5

WHERE NO RIVER FALLS

GLYNN JAMES

First published 2018 by Glynn James

Copyright © Glynn James

The right of Glynn James to be identified as the author of this work has been asserted by him in accordance with the Copyright, Designs and Patents Act 1988.

This is a work of fiction. Names, characters, places, and incidents either are the product of the author's imagination or are used fictitiously. Any resemblance to actual persons, living or dead, events, or locales is entirely coincidental.

All rights reserved. No part of this publication may be reproduced, stored in or introduced into a retrieval system, or transmitted, in any form, or by any other means (electronic, mechanical, photocopying, recording or otherwise) without the prior written permission of the author. Any person who does any unauthorised act in relation to this publication may be liable to criminal prosecution and civil claims for damages.

ISBN: 9781980337591

:: Record Date 04:07:4787 21:00

It's been two nights since I stepped through the portal, and I'm exhausted. This is the first time in the last forty-eight hours that I've managed to find a spot to hide and a chance to sleep.

I remember what JH described, when he arrived in Riverfall, but that was not quite what I found when I got here. The bright light of the portal blinded me for a few moments, as did the change to semi-daylight, I guess. No sooner had I stepped through the portal and into the alleyway – which, thankfully, had remained in the same place – than I had to shove off something that bumped into me and started grasping for me. I pushed it away, unable to see what it was until my eyes re-adjusted, and when I did see what was nearby, I ran, stumbling out into the street beyond the alleyway.

They were everywhere. Shamblers.

The entire street was filled with them, most of them standing perfectly, eerily still. They weren't bunched up, and I think that's the only reason I'm still alive. If I'd walked straight into a pack of them, I suspect I would have been devoured before I even knew what was happening. I dodged one a few feet away from me, as it began to move, and started jogging through the crowd, looking for an opening somewhere – a place to escape the things – but there seemed to be no exit in sight, no matter which direction I ran.

The things were silent as I passed by, but as I moved further along the street, weaving between them, they began to wake up. At first it was only the few that I strayed too close to, but eventually other more distant ones started to stir and awaken.

I had to find somewhere out of their way, and I had to do it fast.

That proved to be more difficult than it sounds. The rough layout of the city beyond the portal, which JH named Riverfall, was basically the same; the same boarded up buildings, still crumbling over time, the same littered streets and the market stalls on the street beyond the alleyway. Despite that, pretty much everything else had changed. There were no street vendors, no hustle of a busy market. The place was devoid of the living, and the state of the streets suggested to me that it had been this way for a while. Rubble from crumbling walls piled up on the pavement, collapsing market stalls blocked the street in several places, and debris and litter gathered in corners and up against doors – any place it could. Whatever had changed in this place had done so long before I arrived there. I judged it to maybe be years, by the state of the decay.

So, I kept moving, passing the run-down market stalls and dodging Shamblers. From what I could see of the remains left rotting there, the market street hadn't been used for years.

It's the strangest city I've ever seen. Even though I was

constantly moving to keep away from the Shamblers, which were quite a worry to me, now they gathered in large numbers as they homed in on me, I still managed to look out across the landscape. There weren't many tall buildings, most being only one or two stories high, and there were some large open spaces that I presume had once been plazas or more market areas. The sprawl of buildings went on and on until it met the outer wall.

Now, I'm pretty sure I read books about city walls back when I was a kid, but they were from something called a medieval period. A lot of the books in Evac City Library were recovered from other worlds, but most of them, or the majority at least, were taken from JH's home world. I remember reading about a period in that world's history called the medieval period, and I marvelled that even back then they wore armoured body suits, except they made them entirely of metal rather than the ablative, synthetic materials the Resistance uses. But the thing that stuck out for me was the castles and fortresses they built.

Well, the walls surrounding the city of Riverfall were like that, only, well, immeasurably bigger. When I first saw the wall in the distance, I thought it was quite close, but I soon realised, as I moved through the city following the more open and unobstructed roads, that the wall was easily five miles away in all directions, and the spot where I'd arrived was roughly in the centre.

I tried blocking up the downstairs of one of the

buildings, using scrap wood that I found, but with no nails or hammer, I was stuck with just jamming stuff into gaps, and that didn't hold off the Shamblers. Soon there were hands poking through the gaps I'd left, and bodies crowded and shoved at each other. I think they numbered in the hundreds at that point, and the sheer volume of them was forcing not only the door to bend inward but the walls to start cracking.

So up onto the upper floor I went, down the fire escape on the other side of the building, and out onto the road behind the house. That did stall them for a while, but within half an hour I had another trail of them following me.

And so it went for two days until I found this old library building leaning up against the outer wall. I'm up on the top floor, some six floors up.

I found the building while heading further out towards the wall, hoping to find some signs of life, hoping to find the small park that JH found the portal to the Ashlands in, but I've no idea where that might be. I was in such a hurry to get away from the Shamblers that I completely forgot to look for signs of my mother's passage. And Ilya? Where was she?

The stairs to the library building would once have run up all six floors, inside a stairwell in the middle of the building, but they seemed to have been destroyed – for the first three floors, at least. Some of the stairs themselves lay in a pile of broken wood at the bottom of the shaft. Fortunately, there was enough metalwork and snapped off wood jutting out that it was an easy climb for me.

Better still, it was an impossible climb for the Shamblers, and they just stopped at the bottom of the stairs and started to congregate there, drifting around aimlessly as soon as I was no longer close.

So I'm taking the uppermost floor to sleep on and using the roof to spy across the city. You really can see everything from up there.

Also, something that has me very curious. The outer wall is easily two hundred feet high. Yeah, no kidding. It's monstrous. Well, this building, all six floors and the roof of it, goes up only two-thirds of the height of the wall, and as I look up, the spire on the top adds another thirty feet.

I'd estimate that the remaining gap between the top of the spire and what looks, I think, to be a walkway on the wall must be seventy feet. It's difficult to make out just what is up there, but I'm almost definite from the overhang of the structure that there is some sort of platform at the top.

Part of the roof of the library building has collapsed, leaving a gap that I could climb up through, out onto the roof. It's flat up there, apart from the spire that rises in the middle, so I can get out and have a look across the city without too much worry about plummeting a hundred feet to the ground and into the mass of dead gathered there.

I need to find some food. I've got maybe six days of

ration packs left, so I'll have to use them sparingly, maybe even half ration myself.

I really could do with something to see across the city with – a telescope or something like that. It's very bright up there – even though I've yet to see the sun – but the mist that drifts over the top of the walls makes it difficult to see very far. I'd say I can see half way across the city and no further than that.

I put down quite a few of the dead in my two-day stint moving from place to place, but they weren't gathered in large numbers like they are now doing at the bottom of the building. I'm going to have to venture out tomorrow, after I've slept, and I think it may take a while to kill them all. Thankfully shredders don't run out of power very quickly, and I'm yet to test how the assault-rifle fires.

I haven't seen Ilya since I stepped through the portal. I hope it's like before and she is just somehow displaced from me. I'm positive that she came through at the same time I did.

It's very odd. I presumed her state was the same as Professor Adler and Rudy's, but maybe it isn't. I don't recall any mention of displacement when JH went through portals with them; in fact, I'm quite sure that there was never an incident, and they were drawn back to him whenever either of them were distanced from him, like there was some link involving the portal key that Ilya and I don't have. Maybe that's where the answer to the mystery lies?

:: Record Date 05:07:4787 07:32

Okay, there's an interesting change in my circumstances this morning.

I woke up early when a blaze of bright light shone through a gap in the ceiling. The light outside doesn't penetrate much of the building inside, thanks to most of the roof still being intact, but like I said, there is one big gaping hole and the light somehow managed to find me through it as I lay in my makeshift bed, which is almost on the opposite side from the gap. It was enough to warm the area I was sleeping in significantly, and I awoke sweating.

It hasn't rained since I arrived. The weather is sort of flat, permanently set in mild spring, and that means I've been neither hot or cold, and the room warming like that was enough to stir me from my sleep.

I've been sleeping a hell of a lot. I don't know if it's the constant eerie feeling about The Corridor or the fact that I was never safe anywhere, and now I'm six floors up in a building that it would be difficult to sneak into, but it's made my tiredness catch up with me.

As usual, I ate half a ration pack and drank some of the remaining water before even moving from my makeshift bed. It's amazing how warm a big pile of books surrounding you can be. I'd never thought of trying it before, and even though pulled up carpets are not particularly comfortable, it's not cold, and they're solid to lie on.

I climbed up onto the roof after finishing my meagre breakfast. I'm still feeling hungry. Maybe that goes with the huge amount of sleep. I don't know. My body seems to be demanding more of me the less I do.

I made my way over to the edge of the roof, to the spot that gave me the best view over the city. I didn't even look down for the start, and I just ignored the inevitable that was still likely to be there, or at least what I believed would still be there. Instead, I stared out over the city, peering as best I could into the distance. I could see a lot of landmarks that are becoming familiar to me, most of which are several miles away.

There's a pair of tall spires, which I think must be somewhere in the centre of the city, and a large area where there are notably taller buildings that face onto a space that is void of buildings. My guess is that it may be the market area, only a few hundred yards from the portal alleyway, though I can't see clearly enough. There aren't any other areas that look open enough to fit the market I ran through on the first day. There is also an incredibly large building maybe a half a mile from that. I've no idea what it's purpose is, but it looms over the rest of the area like some ancient monolith.

I have no idea what direction is north or west, really. You presume that the sun rises and sets the same, but I've been on many worlds where that isn't the case. And it doesn't help that the sun is constantly hidden behind the mist or clouds above.

I've never actually seen the sun in the few days I've been here. Even though it is bright during the day, a heavy layer of clouds blocks the sky. Although there are clear spots amongst the clouds, and sometimes it almost seems for a moment that the sun will burst through them, it never actually does.

So, yeah, this huge building. I'm not sure what it is. It has no features or distinguishing marks that give me a clue as to its function, only that it's easily as tall as this library and much, much larger in area – maybe ten times as much floor space. It also lies not far from the wall, but far enough that it will be quite a trek to get there.

There is a group of massive trees still in bloom far on what I think is the west side, and a monument of some sort near the middle, not far from the market. It was while I was looking at these that I happened to notice that it was all very quiet.

I've had trouble getting off to sleep ever since the first night, even six floors up, and I've even moved my sleeping spot a couple of times to see if it made any difference, but it didn't. The noise of the gathering crowd below, their moans and groans, was loud in the relative quiet of the city, and I found myself looking down to check that they couldn't get up to where I was. Not because I was frightened of them but because of the noise they were making.

At least that was what I told myself.

A dozen or more times I'd decided that I should deal with them, get the shredder out and be done with it, but I was still on edge from my escape from the bunker, and as pathetic as it may sound, I was not quite ready for a confrontation with several hundred walking horrors. But that problem, it seemed, had gone away.

The ground below the library was completely empty of Shamblers. Not a single one in sight. I looked around, scanning the street below and the various streets that lead from it.

Nothing.

I ran to the other side, thinking maybe they'd shifted around to the back of the building or maybe somehow found a way up onto another floor, but they weren't there either.

Panicking, I climbed back down onto the floor below and peered down. It was empty.

I hurried back onto the roof and looked down the streets again, searching for even a sign of one of them. Nothing. They'd all gone, not a single Shambler anywhere.

:: Record Date 05:07:4787 10:15

Heading out to investigate.

There must be answer to why they've gone.

The weather seems more overcast than usual; the brightness has lost its edge.

I did a quick weapon check and grabbed as much stuff as I knew I could carry and still be able to run. I decided to leave some of the equipment that I'd brought with me behind. Even if I find the portal today, I still haven't found Ilya, and I can't leave this place until I find her. So I figured I could leave the heavier bits here and come back for them later. Unless I find a better camp, I'm pretty sure I'll be using the library for a while at least until I find what I'm looking for – both the portal and Ilya. Hell knows how long that may take me.

I am taking a book I found while I was lying there, listening to the drone of the Shamblers and trying to sleep. I found myself staring at the titles of the books. I'd mostly ignored them, but this one seemed newer than the others, and it wasn't bound in leather or cloth like many of the old tomes that line the walls of the building. It wasn't until the light from outside reflected the shiny lettering that I was able to read the title.

A Thesis by Professor Adler.

It didn't register for a few seconds, but then I realised

what I was staring at. I grabbed JH's diary and flicked back, and damn if it wasn't the very same – exactly that – book listed there. This was really the book that Adler wrote, here on a bookshelf on an entirely different world. Or at least I *think* it's an entirely different world.

I'm not totally sure where this is, but I'm pretty sure this isn't Adler's home world. How crazy is that? A total mind-blowing mystery. Obviously some random objects managed to find their way into The Corridor, but I kind of knew how most of that happened, from reading the JH diaries and from knowing how sometimes portals can have a lasting effect on the area around them, even long after they are closed. But this wasn't just a random object in an odd place. This was a book from another world on the shelf of a library in a place that Adler never actually visited.

How did it get here? I have no idea.

Damn it. That one is going to bother me forever.

So, yeah. I took the book. I'll get to read it even though it doesn't belong here. Where the hell does it belong, though?

:: Record Date 05:07:4787 10:30

There was not a single Shambler on the ground floor. A lot of the windows had been broken in and most of the furniture was smashed beyond recognition. When I first arrived, I rushed through the building, trying to find a way to climb up, and I paid little attention to what was down there, but I can remember that some of it had still been intact. But not now. Everything's been trampled. I would imagine that those things wandered around here the whole time, pushing, shoving, trying to find a way up to me, and gradually broke everything. Now the ground floor is just one flat area of squashed rubble and furniture.

I stood in the shade of the main entrance, looking outwards onto the street, watching for any signs of one of them before I stepped out. I wondered if maybe they had gone into the buildings that surround the area, but that just didn't seem right to me.

I know enough from encountering them that they don't have intelligence, as such. They are instinctual beings. Their cognitive brain function disappeared long ago, and they tend to only move in reaction to something changing around them. I've seen entire swarms of them standing perfectly still before, only to move in reaction to a noise nearby or a bright flash of light.

So, something either must've drawn them away or they are just no longer there. I have no doubt that if there had been a fight down here, if other people had been involved, I'd have heard some sort of commotion and surely there would be remnants left behind. And yet there was nothing. Not even a body. They have moved on, gone somewhere else entirely, and it's baffling.

I wish that I could find Ilya. Maybe she'd have some idea. I must find her, so I'm heading back to the market, retracing my steps back to the alleyway. Maybe she arrived at the same time as me but in an adjacent building or nearby street. The buildings lining the market and the alleyways that run off it are so crammed in together that even a short distance could mean an entirely different street. She could have panicked the same way I did. Maybe she ran but in a different direction.

Time to find out.

:: Record Date 05:07:4787 12:00

It's now midday, and I'm sitting on one of the benches. One of the stalls in the market to be precise. Yes, that's right, sitting.

There's nothing here.

No Shamblers, nothing.

Now, I do remember that I didn't kill any of them in the market area. I just left as quickly as I could, figuring that if I shot anything even the low hiss of the shredder may wake up more around me. I shoved that first one away, without killing it, so there wouldn't be any bodies in the market area.

But I did kill some along one of the streets not far from the market, and I've just come back from there, trying to figure out what's going on, but I found no sign of the ones that I'd killed.

This is getting quite eerie. How is it that something that was once dead, then reanimated, then killed, could move again? Sure, maybe a couple of them that I shot went down but weren't destroyed, maybe they weren't true shots, but I know at least a few of my shots were fatal ones.

It's puzzling. I can see the spot where I came through the portal, and I can see the corner of the alleyway where JH would have met...what was his name? The guy sleeping in the trash? I can't remember. I must look that up. I remember he was a ranger – yeah, he was hiding in the trash at the back of the alleyway, I'm sure of it.

I'm going to check some of the other streets nearby for any sign of...well, anything.

:: Record Date 05:07:4787 13:40

Found one single Shambler!

But there's a weirdness about it. This one is somewhat different to the ones I've seen over the last few days. All the ones in this city that I've seen so far were Shambler type A

– that is the sort that were dead and reanimated somehow. You know, nasty, rotten and smelly. You get the image.

But this loner is one of those that this is more like one of the ones that JH described walking about and ignoring him when he stayed at the bus in The Corridor. Shambler type B. They're abominations, and from what I've learned of them, not always dead. Yeah, shudder material. The thing even had its arms reattached in the wrong places – one in the middle of its chest and one on its back.

I caught up to it with my handgun drawn, ready to take it out if necessary; I even called out and then walked around it, keeping my distance, waving my free hand in front of its face.

All it did was stumble past me, completely ignorant of my existence.

Something is not right here.

:: Record Date 05:07:4787 19:00

Still no sign of Ilya, and apart from the single wandering oddness – which I stayed with for half an hour as it wandered in a repeating circuit around four adjoining streets, repeating the same path constantly – I've seen no other signs of life or living death.

I headed back to the library to camp up. Tomorrow, if the situation is the same, I'm gonna start some sort of planned search of the city.

A map. That's what I need. The library must be the best place to start. If I can't find a map of the city, at least there should be plenty of paper to make one from. A grid plan is what is needed, the same kind we use when we do systematic loot and tech salvage hunts in ruined settlements when we're out on expeditions. I can do the same to find the portal.

:: Record Date 06:07:4787 08:32

Today I ventured further out from the library once more. First, I went back to the market again to see if the single Shambler was still around, but I couldn't find it. The place is now completely empty, not a living or undead thing around – not even a bird. Come to think of it, I've not seen a single bird since I got here, which is strange. You'd think there would be some living on the roofs of the buildings, scavenging like they do, but there is nothing.

None of this makes any sense to me.

I started searching through some of the abandoned shops, or what I thought may have been shops. Most of them are off the streets near the market, and I hoped I'd find something interesting hidden away in one of them, so I searched quite a few – maybe three dozen – before I gave up. I found very little in the way of supplies in any of them, and there was certainly no food of any kind. Whoever lived in this city before I arrived seems to have stripped the place quite thoroughly.

Eventually, I headed further away from the market and found something that was a bit closer to what I needed. I remembered a section of JH's diary, and how he had had to get past the barrier wall that separated one area of the city from another. It had been defended by guards, if I remember correctly, but not anymore. The reason for the barrier has gone from my mind, and I wonder if JH even figured that out when he was here. I must have a look at the diary when I get back to the library.

Finding the barrier here was a relief. I was beginning to think I'd ended up…I don't know, in some weird alternate version of the city. I was also starting to think I would never find a clue that might lead me in the right direction. I could spend weeks, months, or years searching this city for the location of the portal and I might never find it, but now that I've found the barrier, it might lead to some clues. At least it's a place to start from. JH crossed this barrier at some point and headed into an area even more ruined. The buildings beyond what's left of the barrier certainly fit that description.

What this means is I'm back on the on the trail. JH went this way, and that's where I will need to follow. I guess I just need to find somewhere reasonably safe to build a new temporary camp. Preferably somewhere up high. It's a strange construction – the barrier, I mean. It seems to almost split an entire section of the city off from the rest and for no apparent reason. I'm going to head back to the library now, before it gets darker, but I'm making a mental note of the fastest route back to this area.

:: Record Date 07:07:4787 03:32

Woke in the middle of the night to find that the temperature had dropped significantly. I know this sounds irrelevant, but most nights here are quite mild. Even though the sun doesn't show its face in the day, and the moon is barely visible at night, it's not cold. The weather doesn't alter much at all, really. I've not seen any sign of rain. But last night I awoke to a sharp, freezing wind blowing through the building, and worse than that, I could hear the noises outside once more. I went up onto the roof to look down and there they all were, gathered at the foot of the building. Hundreds of Shamblers.

So after...what? Three days? It seems that they're back again. I can't figure out how this could be. I didn't see any of them in my two days wandering around the city, apart from that single one, near the market, that couldn't even detect me when I waved my hands in front of it. There is something very odd going on here.

They were here, then they were gone without a trace at all, and now they're back, crowded around the bottom of the library. I'm pretty sure there is more of them, too, and even more approaching slowly along the streets. At this rate

I'll end up with a Shambler singularity right under my feet. They are in their hundreds. I don't know. At a guess I'd say there are at least three hundred of them out there.

Other than worrying about the job of getting rid of the damn things, this also got me thinking about the change in weather and the strange appearance of the Shamblers – and, more importantly, their disappearance and re-appearance. I wonder if it's something to do with the weather change? I can't explain where they went while the weather was more overcast, but I have to admit it is very odd.

Before I went to sleep, the sky was clear. It wasn't grey. It wasn't as cold, and there wasn't a single creature as far as I could see, not along any of the streets or in the buildings that I can see into – which is most of the ones with windows, since the glass has long been broken in most of them. That's how it's been for a few days now, ever since my first night in the library. Yet now I wake up and the sky is grey again, and it's bitter cold, and there is a roiling in the clouds.

Shamblers don't just go wandering off together to hide and then come back – at least not unless there is something that draws their attention away from potential food. I heard nothing like that. And for them to come back again a few days later? It's just weird.

I could swear that I even recognise some of them.

Anyway, oddness aside, I have deal with them. I can't leave without shooting them all, otherwise they will just follow me around, drawing more and more of them to me.

So that's this morning's task. I'm going to try out this assault rifle and see how it performs in comparison to my old sniper rifle or the handguns.

:: Record Date 07:07:4787 09:40

Wow. Just wow, is all I can say.

My new assault shredder is probably one of the most efficient weapons I've ever seen. It's fire rate is off the scale in comparison to others, and the accuracy…well, if I could modify it for range, it would be shocking.

It's a bit disheartening to think of all the hours I spent fine-tuning my old rifle only to lose it, but this thing is far more powerful, and the battery use is wickedly efficient. It's not like anything I've seen. It's just amazing. It fires much faster than I can really control, so I had to tinker with that a little and found out how to fire it with short bursts. I'm pretty sure it must have been designed to fire from a mount or something.

I've not seen anyone carrying anything like this. I even think may be able to customise this thing to use even less juice, if I had the time and a workshop to do it in. Something to think about for the future, if ever I find a place. I haven't really tested the range to its fullest, but I bet this baby can push beyond my old rifle with some work.

There were a lot more Shamblers below me than I thought, but, well, let's just say ten minutes and they were no longer a problem. There aren't any wandering around at a distance to aim at anymore. They all seemed to have gathered about the bottom of the library. But, since I saw quite a lot of them around the city before they all disappeared, I'm betting they are back there too.

Back to the weather changes and the weirdness. I know the strangest of things happened to JH when he was down in The Corridor, but I've never heard of anything quite like this. Maybe it's just my imagination. Maybe they really did wander off and hide somewhere, but I find that very hard to believe. Anyway, with this new weapon, I'm not really worried about heading out anymore, as long as I keep my distance and I'm careful. I should be fine. Hopefully.

I'm waffling again.

:: Record Date 07:07:4787 20:21

Noticed something strange this evening as I was standing on the top floor of the library looking out over the city. I've been doing this every night, at least for a few hours, maybe in the hope that I'll see some signs of life in the distance. You know, a light or something – some movement. But so far, as the days have passed by, I've seen nothing.

Until tonight!

It was in a place I wasn't expecting to see it. There were still no signs of movement across the city. Not a single pinpoint of light. But on a whim – and it must have been the most coincidental of timings – I glanced upward and behind me at the vast wall that surrounds the city. I've contemplated that wall quite a lot since arriving here. It dominates the horizon in all directions, at least as far as I can see. I can't see the far end of the city from here, but I can see the wall on at least three sides, though what must be about half of it is obscured by the distant haze that seems to constantly sit over the city. It blocks out any kind of horizon – meaning the world.

The people who lived in this city must have had a strange sense of perception. I think if I lived in such a place for too long it would distort how I saw the world. To not be able to see as far as the horizon is somehow strange, and it doesn't help that you never really see the sun or any moons, or even distant stars. The world here seems to be encased behind these walls and under the haze.

Anyway, my curiosity constantly touches upon what lies beyond barrier. I think about the distance between the top of the spire and the platform above. The library is built against the wall, so there's no gap for me to fall into, but still, to fall that kind of distance, I could seriously injure myself. Sure, I'd heal over time, purely because of the serum that runs through my blood, and I'd recover from most injuries I could end up with, but it would leave me stuck there, probably incapacitated, for a good while. What happens if a bunch of Shamblers turn up and I can't move? Well, the end, that's what. Also, the fall could still kill me. There's only so much that nanites can stitch back together.

The problem isn't the overall height of the wall, really; it's the seventy-foot extra between the top of the library and the platform above. How to get up there? The wall isn't smooth, but also there is a lip at the top, where the ledge is. How would I get around it?

This is the sort of thing that goes through my mind when I look up there, and it was the same this evening, except, as I looked up, I saw a small flicker of movement not far along the platform.

There was something up there, a shadow against the dim glow of the sky. I couldn't make out what it was that was moving, but it was making its way slowly along the platform. Could it be possible to live up there instead of down here? It would be safer than the living down in the city, where those creatures wandered. But how would you survive up there?

Something has. Something was moving around on the top of the parapet and along the platform as I watched. Then the movement was gone, the shadow disappearing to merge with the rest of the darkness. It made me uneasy for the rest the evening, thinking that I was being watched the whole time. I eventually fell into an uneasy sleep in my makeshift bed among the books and carpets.

:: Record Date 08:07:4787 01:15

I'm going up there. It's decided.

I climbed up out of the top floor onto the roof, made my way across to the wall, and I now know that I don't need the rope to get up there, at least not one as long as I thought. I'm going to need something to hook over the parapet when I get up there, because there is an overhang of about four feet, and I dread the idea of hanging up there and not being able to get back down again, so a rope may still be the answer. I may be able to climb around the parapet on the way up, but getting back around it and onto the wall... No. Too risky.

Quite what I'll do with that I don't know. I'll come up with something. But I'm definitely going up there to find out who is moving around.

:: Record Date 08:07:4787 06:51

Slept on it and woke up staring at the curtains hanging from the windows. They are thick, heavy drapes coloured red, mostly, but worn and faded in many places. Most of these curtains are like tapestries, with strange pictures on them depicting festivals or other kinds of celebration or gathering.

It was as I lay there, staring at one such image, that I realised that part my answer was right in front of me, hanging from every single window.

I needed a rope, and there, hanging by the side of each set of heavy drapes was a pull rope to draw the curtains back.

:: Record Date 08:07:4787 13:20

Now it's lunchtime, and I've spent much of the morning gathering the pull ropes and hooking the drapes over the hooks on the wall to stop it getting too draughty in the building. I just ate one of my few remaining rations, and now I have the wonderful task of somehow stitching all these bits of rope together. It may take some time. I also need some form of hook to grapple over the top of the parapet.

One task at a time.

:: Record Date 08:07:4787 15:20

I ended up with about fifty feet of rope and a lasso hoop about five feet across by the end of the afternoon. I think that should be enough. Shame I didn't have more of the rope. I wondered if I could find some somewhere else.

With that thought, I rushed to the edge of the library and looked at some of the other buildings. None of the ones nearby had the same sort of curtains, but across the city, about half a mile away, I could see what I thought must have been a church. Next to that were a bunch of other older looking buildings, much bigger than most in the city, not too far from the centre. Maybe a hall of some sort? It was getting dark, so I decided not to head out straight away, but that's where I'm heading tomorrow.

:: Record Date 09:07:4787 12:13

Found what I needed and more. It's midday, and I'm currently standing in the centre of what must have been the city's church – or maybe even cathedral, from the size of it. A lot of the wooden pews have been taken away, though some of them still lie shattered on the ground. At least three quarters of them have disappeared. Why? Maybe somebody used them for firewood?

More importantly, though, every window has those same huge tapestry curtains with draw ropes, and there are more here than there were in the library. I'm going to spend the rest of the afternoon collecting what I can.

:: Record Date 09:07:4787 22:18

It's night again, and I'm back up on top of the library, looking out over the city. I still keep gazing out, hoping I'll see a light, like I have been doing every evening. But after a few minutes this evening I got distracted and found myself staring up at the parapet above, searching for movement once more, but there was nothing tonight.

I have more than enough rope. I'm now in possession of

at least a hundred feet of it, though I need to tie it all together. What it does mean is that I don't have to climb the spire on the top of the library. I'm not going to be able to throw this rope up so high, all the way to the top, so my first trip will be to climb the wall as far as I can get, with the rope over my shoulder, and then hope to throw the loop over a section of the parapet.

:: Record Date 10:07:4787 19:22

The crazy things we do to satisfy curiosity.

I think nearly all the most dangerous things I've ever done in my life have all been just to find an answer to something, and it's rarely been something so important that I should risk my life on it.

The climb up the wall was certainly a little hair-raising. I Slipped a couple of times, but fortunately there are crevasses between the massive stones the wall is built from, and the gaps are wide enough to shove your whole hand in, or even a foot, let alone just hold on to. Both times I slipped I had a decent enough grip, but it still made my stomach churn as the world below loomed at me, threatening to swallow me up. After struggling to throw the loop over the parapet for about fifteen minutes, thinking that my arms were going to give up at any moment, I finally managed to catch it. It was with some nerves that I let go and hung from the rope.

It creaked a little, and I could feel some give as the knots tightened. I should probably have tested it before I decided to go ahead and use it, but hey, it was too late now.

It only took another few seconds to haul myself up over the parapet and onto the platform behind it. I was out of breath by the time I got up there and sat leaning against the wall on the inside of the platform, staring across the flat surface.

It was a two-level platform. The lower one looked out over the city and then there were sets of steps leading up onto a higher platform that must look outside the city. Looking in either direction, I could see that there were no towers anywhere. That hadn't occurred to me from the ground. This platform just ran endlessly around the city. Maybe there are towers further round? I don't know, but I certainly couldn't see any. I also couldn't see anyone up there or any signs that someone had passed this way. No makeshift camps, no discarded junk blowing in the wind.

The wind. My god. The wind up there was a constant gale across the top of the platform. My face and hands were soon cold, and I eventually took shelter behind one of the walls.

After a while I went to look out over the wall and see what was beyond. I climbed the dozen or so stairs onto the top platform before walking to the edge. I felt a little dizzy as the ground loomed at me from the other side of the wall.

Outside the city is not quite what I'd expected. I think I

was anticipating a barren and dead world, possibly scorched, or at least something so terrifying and dangerous that they would need to build such a wall. However, all I can make out is a forest as far as the eye can see. It starts about a hundred yards outside the city wall.

Massive trees, probably half as tall as the wall in some places, cover the landscape to the horizon. They must be ancient, to have grown so tall, and they have strange purplish leaves so that the whole area beyond the wall has an odd tint to it. Is it autumn? Maybe in summer the whole forest would be lush and green. Though something in the back of my mind suggested what I was looking at was permanent, unchanging.

I looked straight down the wall to the open ground below. Something moved down there, and I squinted, trying to focus on what it was. Then realised that most of the ground below the front of the wall wasn't flat ground and it wasn't rocky.

The whole area was moving, swaying like a sea, and then a face looked up at me from the blur of movement. My stomach churned, and I took an involuntary step back from the wall.

It wasn't the ground at all that I was looking at, but a sea of Shamblers all the way up to the outside of the wall. The one that stared up to the sky at me reached out with its hand, pointing at me as though accusing me of something, then it howled and other faces turned to the sky.

More howls came from the mass, until the sound echoed off the wall. I stumbled further backwards, not wanting to witness that sight anymore.

So that is why they built the outside wall. Even though the forest was beautiful and endless, a sea of Shamblers awaited them. Their entire world must have been overrun by the things.

I stood there, leaning against one of the inner parapet walls, feeling my heart thumping in my chest.

"Will you throw yourself to your death, now?" asked a voice from nearby.

I spun around, surprised to hear anyone. Even though I had climbed up there looking for whoever it was that had moved around in the darkness at night, at that moment I hadn't expected anyone. Only twenty feet away stood a short figure dressed in ragged clothing.

I reached for my handgun. I'd only brought the one up with me – I hadn't wanted to risk dropping my rifle.

The figure waved its hand casually and spoke again. "No need for that," it said. "I mean no harm, and I'm certainly not intending to throw you from the wall, if that's what you're worried about."

The voice sounded male, but the tattered hood obscured my view of the person's face.

"It's just that most who see what lies beyond the wall

cannot cope with the vision, and more than a few have ended themselves in despair."

"Why is the wall so tall?" I asked, regaining my composure and taking my hand from my side. If the man did charge, I was far enough away that I was confident I could draw and fire before he reached me.

"To keep what is outside from getting in," he said simply. Then he drew his hood away from his face and squinted out towards the forest.

"To keep out Shamblers?" I asked. "A bit excessive just for that, isn't it?"

The man frowned. "Shamblers? Is that what you call those who have died and risen once more? The ones some fell wind brought back to walk in the world of the living."

"Yes," I said. "at least where I come from we call them that."

"Hmm," said the man. "Shamblers. I had not heard that term for them, but I suppose it is a fitting one. I must say, of course, that they are not the real problem. Or the reason for the wall being as tall as it is."

"What do you mean?"

"I'd suggest you take another look," he answered. "Though be careful of the wind. I'd hate for you to fall. I've had few people to converse with in all these years, and I'd be disappointed if you were to join the rest of them that threw themselves from the wall."

I edged back toward the outer parapet, held onto the rough stone wall, and looked over the edge, puzzled. All I could see was the tiny heads of the dead things on the ground, whose numbers must have been in the thousands. Of course, there could be a million of them down there, hidden by the strange purple mass of the forest.

"You really don't see them, do you?" he said. I hadn't heard him move, but he now stood a few feet away along the wall.

"I see the creatures below," I said, "but that's all."

"And what of the forest?" he asked.

"Of course. Obviously I see that."

I peered into the forest but couldn't see what it was that I was missing. Something hidden in there? I watched, momentarily puzzled, until I finally caught a glimmer of something that wasn't right. The creatures below weren't the only ones moving. The forest itself swayed in a strange, pulsing motion, and it wasn't the kind of movement that was caused by wind. The trees shook occasionally, as though trying to throw off their autumn leaves.

Then one of the trees moved.

"Yes," said the man. He was looking directly at me, "Finally he sees."

It wasn't a forest at all, for there were no trees. The

creatures below, now that I could make out some details, may have looked like trees but they weren't. I could see thick, warped branch-like arms with tentacles at the end, each of which was covered in a mass of leafy protrusions that opened and closed constantly. The main body of the creatures was like a trunk, but pale in colour, like…a mushroom? Were these things some form of massive fungus?

"What the hell are they?"

"Indeed," he said. "What are they? That we've never really known, only that in the old years before this city was built, the only place where people could find refuge was below ground, where the creatures could not reach them. Some of the old stories tell of how they spread across the old world by casting spores to the wind. They ravaged cities, tearing the buildings to the ground. Finally, the remnants of whoever came before us built this place, with its wall tall enough that the spores could not make their way in. They cannot rise high into the air, you see, and travel low to the ground, swept along by the wind, but this wall has more than its height to deter them.

"I am old," he continued. "But I'm not so old that I that I knew those folk, or how they could build something the creatures could not tear down or climb. These walls are strange. I sometimes wonder if they are almost alive themselves. They're certainly not built from any material that I could name. Many of those creatures make attempts up the wall, both…Shamblers and the tentacled ones that have no name. It's an interesting sight to see when the wall fights back and defends itself."

He was quiet for a while.

"Is that why you came up here? To see what lies beyond?"

"No, actually. I suppose it did cross my mind, but I came because I saw movement up here, and I've not seen anyone in the city since I got here."

"Ah. I gave myself away, then."

"I guess."

"I must admit I have been watching you. You are a rare visitor to this place. There is no one in the world outside that I know of, so you do not come from here."

"No," I said. "I arrived through a portal. A gate, of sorts."

He frowned at me. "What manner of gate?"

"Erm…a door from another place. Another world. My name is Connor." I held out my hand to shake his, but he just peered at me, still frowning.

"I am Allon. And what do you mean, another world?"

I shrugged. "Another world, not that much different to any other, I guess. My world is called Gaia."

"Like any other? There are many that are inhabited?"

Allon asked.

"Yes. Thousands that we know of. Probably a million we don't," I said.

"How very strange. Intriguing."

"Do you live here alone?" I asked

"Yes and no. It was not always so. But I have done for many a year, now. There used to be a lot of us that watched the walls, but as the population below diminished over the years, some chose to move on. Some have died and never been replaced. I have come close to moving on myself, a few times, but there are still a few stragglers living in the ruins, and we on the walls vowed to give our lives to watch over them. And so it is I still stand vigil here. The last of my kind, to watch the last of theirs."

"Are there many people left?"

"You ask a lot of questions of me, and I am tired," he said.

"I'm sorry, I just haven't spoken to anyone in a while."

"It is fine. Come. We can't stay here. It's too cold to be on the platform for too long. Come."

I followed him along the platform on the top of the wall for only a few minutes. He was moving quickly, but I could hear laboured breathing. Eventually we came to a set of stairs that led from the platform down into the wall itself, and from there the stairs led down to a trio of chambers along a small corridor.

The first we passed seemed to be a seating area with torn old sofas and chairs. I was surprised to see a television screen upon a table. I hadn't considered that this society was advanced enough for that kind of technology.

We moved past what looked like a kitchen and into a much larger room. More sofas were set up in a square around the centre, and beyond that were some desks with hard wooden chairs. Covering most of the walls were shelves crammed with books and ornaments.

"This is my home, of sorts," said Allon.

"It's…warm."

He laughed. "Yes. I couldn't think of much else to say about it, either. The door keeps danger away, and it is indeed warm. I spend much time up on the wall, walking and watching both sides. It's good to hide away somewhere not so breezy come nightfall. There are more than a dozen of these places around the wall, all much the same, though I prefer this one. Come and sit. I will make some tea and you can ask more of your questions, if you must. There is a much easier way down from the wall from here, so you need not worry about climbing down in the dark."

"A way down?" I asked, thinking also that it would be a way up.

"Yes, yes. The stairs." He moved over to one side of the room as I found a seat on one of the sofas. A moment later

I heard the click and the bubbling of a kettle.

"You have electricity here?"

"Yes, we have all the luxuries." He chuckled to himself. "The city used to, of course. Electric lights and heating. After the upheaval, there was no one to run the power station any longer, so it stopped working, and the lights went out. I still have power via solar panels on the parapet, though. Well, in most of the rest-stops I do. Not all."

"What was this upheaval?"

"Ah, yes. The Dark One came, maybe three decades ago. Many died in the days after, not because of the Dark one, but because they disagreed. It was a civil war, of sorts. Terrible to watch."

"Did it last long?" I was thinking of the time after JH passed through and when my mother must have come here.

"A few years. But many fled through the portal left behind by the Dark One, some of them claiming it led to a safer place. Many of course did not believe, and they stayed. The Dark One was followed later, by more of its kin, and they took up residence in part of the city. They built a fort as well."

"Stygians?" I asked. I presumed by the Dark One he meant Nua'lath.

"I do not know that name. Stop interrupting me." He brought over a hot cup of tea and I took it. I felt the warmth with such a relief; I had no idea I'd missed hot food or drink.

"Sorry," I said.

"Another stranger came, years later, and banded the remaining groups together. They fought the...Stygians – or whatever you call them – and also fled through the gate. But some were left behind. Not many, but some. And more Stygians came to hold the metal castle. I suspect those left behind would leave if they could. They spy on the Stygians often enough."

I waited for more of the tale, but no more came.

"You only stay for the few that remain?"

"Yes, as I said. Maybe if they manage to leave I will leave."

"But where? Where would you go."

"I would follow them through once they were gone."

"Can't you join them?"

He shook his head. "Not while they are inside the walls. It is our vow not to interfere, to avoid contact. We're not of their kind, really, as keepers of the wall. We were never meant to be among them, only to watch them. Before you ask, no, I cannot tell you where they hide. It would be interfering."

"I wasn't expecting you would."

"No, maybe not, but I've noticed that you have not yet

met those who remain. You must know, then, that it is not my place to say."

"You can't even tell me roughly where they are?" I asked.

He shook his head. "Alas, no. I know little of you enough to think that you are not a threat to them. But a vow is a vow, and I will not break mine. I cannot guide you towards those whom I watch over."

I sighed, disappointed.

"What reason have you for being here, anyway?

"I was trying to find the gate that leads out of here. My mother travelled through, many years ago."

He seemed to ponder this while we sat in silence.

"You will find it in the north of the city, though I think you will find there are those who would keep you from it. At this time, those…Stygians still hold their metal castle. They won't leave, it seems. It annoys me, but I am an old man and couldn't do much to help, even if I was allowed to."

"I may be able to help them leave," I said. "If I knew who they were and where the portal was."

"Maybe," he said, nodding. "Maybe you should pursue that end? I have, of course, told you too much already – that they even exist, for example – but, like you, I have not spoken to anyone for a long time. I forget myself. But enough for now. I am old, and tired, and I need to sleep.

Make yourself comfortable, if you wish to stay here tonight. If you leave, use the stairs. It's quite a trek down. Make sure you close the door when you go out."

With that, he pulled a sheet over himself, curled up on the sofa he had been sitting on, and was snoring within seconds. I looked around, found a similar cover, and settled down.

:: **Record Date 11:07:4787 09:10**

Allon had gone when I awoke. I don't remember lying there for long, so I must have fallen asleep as quickly as he had. I gathered my things and headed through the other two rooms but found them empty. The door opened out onto stairs that led in either direction. For a moment I wondered if I should go up, back onto the platform again, and maybe try to find the old man, but I guessed that if he had gone alone then that was probably what he wanted. I closed the door, as he instructed, and headed down the stairs.

It was quite a way down, and the route led back in the opposite direction, heading back towards where I climbed up. At the end I found only a single door on the right side. I pushed it open and was surprised to find myself looking out onto the second floor of the library. Damn him! I laughed. He had probably not only watched me from the platform but could easily have come down here to the library to sneak about as well. I pushed the door shut and found no handle on the other side. It simply closed to leave a smooth wall.

Damn. Should have looked for some way to get back in there. I searched, pushing aside books that lined the walls nearby, but couldn't find an outside trigger to re-open the door. I'm sure there must be one somewhere.

Found my rope had been cut and was sitting in a pile on the roof. I guess I'll need to do the climb again if I want to get back up there. I wonder why he cut it?

:: Record Date 11:07:4787 10:01

Based on what I'd seen from the wall, and Allon's brief directions, I wandered further into the northern part of the city today, probably further than I should have. Although having the library as base means relative safety – at least from the Shamblers – it also means I've limited my ability to explore very far.

I was heading to the far north of the city, taking it street by street. The library, from what I can gather, is almost as far east as you can go. I left at about what I would estimate to be 10am in the morning, and I passed the market area at about midday. From there, I tried to head almost directly north, though the streets didn't always allow me to.

Eventually, I turned a corner to find a section of the barricade. I hurried along the street, not really paying much attention to the buildings I was passing and climbed up onto it.

This was what I came for. To find the barrier and hopefully locate another safehouse in this area. I'd then move there and be able to explore the other side of the barrier easier. At least that was the plan. The barrier was maybe twenty feet tall, with a platform fifteen feet up a set of rough stairs, and had been built from what looked like vehicle parts and scrap sheet metal – as was most of the barricade.

I slowed as I reached the steps, wondering for a moment if there was chance that anyone still manned the defence. When JH crossed it was guarded, but I doubted that it would be now. I wasn't taking any chances though, so I crouched down by the platform, hiding at the top of the steps for a few moments before I cautiously inched forward, peering both ways.

No sign of anyone. I peered over the barricade. It was exactly as JH described it. This part of the city – I'm calling it the north, because it's difficult to judge directions in this place without the sun or the stars at night, and I have no compass – was a lot more ruined than the southern half, where I had been exploring so far.

There was a large open space, almost entirely empty of buildings between the two, like some sort of no man's land that had been blasted flat. Maybe a hundred yards of rough ground stretched away from the barricade before the ruins began once more.

I could see from the outlines of bricks and broken rubble that this gap had probably once also been streets and buildings at some point, but little remained. This was where JH had crossed, sprinting away from the barricade as the guards fired upon him.

No guards here now.

I turned to look back in the direction of the library, or at least roughly where I thought it would be, and spotted the broken spire in the very distance. I could only see part of the top floor, and that explained why I couldn't see this barricade from even up there. The top floor of the library still wasn't high enough to see over the buildings in the way, and most of the barricade would be obscured by the rows of buildings through which it cut – quite literally, in some spots.

As I looked in both directions down the barricade, I could see where the walkway cut straight through a row of buildings. There were walls either side of the intersecting house, but there was a section completely missing, knocked away, maybe.

I started to walk, choosing what I considered to be west, thinking I could just go a little way – half a mile or so – to see if there really were any signs of people, but after ten minutes of walking, I'd still seen nothing. I came across a section of the barrier that had collapsed, leaving a hole at least ten feet across. It convinced me that no one had been here for years. If they had, then surely they would have maintained the wall? I tried to think back to what JH described on the other side. There had been refugees or outcasts living in the ruins, and I vaguely remembered his conversation with them.

Had there been any mention of more Shamblers? I couldn't remember. I don't think so. I would need to check the book.

A lot of the day had already passed by this time, and I needed to think about turning back in a couple of hours. I needed to find my next safehouse fast, otherwise it would be another day of walking all the way there and back, leaving little time to explore. I'd never catch the trail of JH or my mother at that rate. It made me nervous, though, the idea of leaving the library and its relative safety.

Time to start house hunting.

:: Record Date 11:07:4787 19:42

A street away from where I started, I found my ideal place. There are half a dozen houses in the row that would have been fine, but the one I chose was the best furnished and still reasonably undamaged by looting and the weather. I'd say someone must have used it as a base before, though not too recently, because there were bolts on all the doors. The ground floor is well boarded up, and the stairs have been replaced by a ladder. Someone went to some trouble here.

It will do.

Time to head back to the library and get some sleep before I haul it out of that area for good. I'm tempted to see if I can meet up with Allon again, but we'll see. I guess after fifteen years I have as much time as I want – except for the finite supply of food, that is.

:: Record Date 11:07:4787 21:37

I've been robbed.

Everything is gone. Well, nearly everything. All the stuff I left behind at the library.

My second pack with the extra supplies, my spare batteries, and who knows what else. Gone.

So, this leaves me with two thoughts. Either someone else has tracked down my base in the library or Allon wasn't as trustworthy as I thought. I'm not convinced of the latter. Now I know that there are other people in the city, I have it in mind that they must have seen me coming and going from the library, and waited until the timing was right, then made their raid.

But what if Allon had told them I was here? No, I'm not convinced. He said it was his job to not interfere. Can't get more interfering than tipping someone off.

The only thing they haven't taken is JH's diary, which was lying next to my makeshift bed. Of course, to whoever it was that robbed the place, the diary would just be another book. Thankfully it was still lying were I left it.

Damn. Damn. Damn.

I checked my equipment, looking over what little inventory I still had left. One spare battery for each shredder, including the rifle, but that's all out of the dozen or more I had. These things are meant to last the years, but it meant that I only had three chances of failure.

Worse, I barely had any food left. I left a whole bunch of rations here, thinking no one would find them where I'd hidden them. But they did. I took an extra day of food and water with me when I went out, so that leaves me with just that – just one day's worth of food left.

The other week or two of ration packs were in the other bag, and that was now gone. I did look around, just in case some of it had been left behind, unnoticed, but no such luck. Since arriving, other than the Shamblers and Allon, there's been no sign of people moving around, or watching me from the ruins, but that doesn't mean they're not there.

Which means they are probably watching me right now, and I have no idea where from. They could be anywhere. I wish I had Ilya with me. She'd be able to help me search, probably without risk of being attacked. What's worse is that in that pack were the other two shredder guns. Whoever took my stuff may not be familiar with how to use them, but there is also a chance they might be. That means they could be armed with weapons as deadly as those I carry.

I'm leaving now.

No time to prepare the other safehouse; I have to move out. It's frustrating. I spent all those days fleeing from the Resistance, and now, just after I shook them off, I'm running again, and this time from an enemy that I don't know. It may be that they could be friendly, and just took my stuff because the opportunity was there, but I doubt that. This place must be difficult to survive in, and that means I can't judge what extent they will go to.

:: Record Date 11:07:4787 23:36

I'm sure they are following me, but I've not seen movement anywhere. I'm getting paranoid – seeing shadows move across windows, through gaping holes in the sides of buildings. It must just be my imagination. I've moved quickly, not stopping. It's pitch black, out here.

It did occur to me to just travel a few streets, find a hiding place, and sleep, because I was already tired, but if whoever stole my gear was nearby, they could easily track me down and then I would be in trouble.

Fortunately, there are no Shamblers around.

:: Record Date 12:07:4787 00:18

And I was doing so well.

I had the barrier in my sights, not far in the distance, when the first of the things stumbled out of an alleyway about thirty yards ahead of me. It was right after I had to slow down, catch my breath, and wait for a slight dizzy spell to pass. I must have been pushing myself too hard.

I stood still on the path and hoped that the first creature wouldn't spot me, but it was already heading in my direction. Yes, you guessed it – a Shambler. This one limped, dragging a deformed leg behind it. I lifted my rifle and aimed, but then several more stumbling out from the same alleyway distracted me. I glanced around to check other movement and spotted more across the street.

I looked behind me. The intersection that I'd just crossed, barely a minute ago, was bustling with dark shadows – at least a dozen of them. I started firing, and the one that had limped fell but continued to crawl towards me.

It was no good. If I stayed here for too long, firing, the flash of the weapon, even without much noise, would draw the attention of others. There was no telling how many might be already on their way or within distance of spotting the flash. Even with a weapon that doesn't technically ever run out of ammunition, one man can only fight off so many of these things. Plus, the weapon itself could start to overheat if I fired it too many times in such a short period.

Then it would just stop working until the temperature dropped below safe levels.

So, here I am up on the roof once more, only a hundred yards away from the barrier. This is as far as I can get. I think the ladder attached to the side of the building must have been part of a fire escape at one point. Fortunately, it didn't lead all the way up, and I did have to climb a drain pipe for another ten feet to get past the top floor and clamber up onto the rooftop. That should make it nearly impossible for them to follow me up here, but as I suspected, there's a lot of them. In fact, the entire street below me is now rammed.

Any time that strange shift theory wants to kick in, you know, would be good. *Now* would be very good. That's what happened when I was dizzy, wasn't it? It must be. I shifted again.

:: Record Date 12:07:4787 01:35

I was sitting on the roof, beginning to shiver with the cold, when I saw a flicker in the far distance. It was to the north, as I'd suspected it would be, and, as Allon had said, over the barrier and the open ground, far into the ruins. I can just make out the varying colours as they dance across the walls of the buildings nearby, but it's so dark that it shines like a beacon, multicoloured waves flickering across windows and walls. I tried to pinpoint something nearby, maybe a building or other recognisable landmark, something for me to aim for when daylight comes, but the glare of the portal was messing with the shadows and silhouettes, making it difficult to focus on the buildings.

It must be the portal. If it was still active, as I expected it would be, it would shine that brightly. I'm sure of it. That is where I need to go.

As I sat on the roof, waiting for daylight – or maybe just a shift back so that those things disappeared – I started wondering why I hadn't seen the glow of the portal before. I've been up in the library, higher than most buildings, and could see a long way, but still I'd seen nothing as bright as this.

I turned to look back at the buildings in the direction of where the library should be and discovered something very strange. Even though it's dark, there is still a little ambient light from the sky, and without the interruption of the portal, I could see faint outlines of the rooftops of buildings, all the way to the wall, which I can see as a thick, dark line on the horizon, and I can almost make out where the library should be, but it's not there. It's almost as though I can only see so far before everything is veiled.

That would explain it! If I can't even see the library from here, then there was no way I was going to see the light from the portal from there. Between the strange shifts in weather, the appearance and disappearance of the Shamblers, and this odd distance blindness, this is almost as strange a place as The Corridor.

Good news, though. At least I know where I'm going. I can only hope that really *is* the portal to the north. I only have the slight problem of getting off this roof. The entire street below his filled with Shamblers who seem intent on standing there and staring at me. There must be a thousand of them.

:: Record Date 12:07:4787 02:11

Well, that could have been stupidest thing I have done to date, and it should have gone terribly, terribly wrong. Several times I managed to fall asleep on the roof. That was the first thing. When I woke up, I'd slid halfway down the tiles and was close to toppling into the street. That would have ended things rather quickly. I didn't, though, and after a few panicked moments, I scrambled back up onto the peak of the roof.

It was then that I realised I couldn't hang around for the shift to happen or for the things below to go away. They were all still down in the street, staring up at me and moaning.

I looked around for ways out. The next roof was a good thirty feet away. There was no way I was going to jump the gap. The house that stopped my progress had collapsed inwards, and most of its roof now lay on the ground floor, but it still had outer walls. The problem was they were crumbling, and only ten feet high in some places, and it didn't look very stable.

Hoping to find some way of getting down, I walked back along the rooftops, heading toward the end of the street. before the horde caught up with me. Even though they move quite slowly, they move swiftly enough that by the time I reached the end of the row, and considered climbing down the ladder, they were nearly at the corner once more. I dangled my legs down and was going to drop onto the ladder, but the Shamblers were already stumbling around the corner. By the time I climbed down, I'd be kicking at them to get to the ground.

I didn't bother. It was too risky.

I had managed to draw many of them down the street, though, and it emptied the ruined building below, allowing me to get a better look at the interior. If I used my rope, I could lower myself down far enough to get onto the wall below. Hopefully I would be able to cross by staying on the top of the wall. I would have to risk getting across crumbling masonry to the other side, where I could see a drain pipe leading up the outside of the next building.

It was too high to reach from the wall, and I would have to depend on climbing a section of what would have been the inside of the house. There were two floors of collapsed floorboards and bricks jutting out from the far wall — enough to make the climb if it didn't collapse on me.

It was decided. I went back to the chimney that I had tied

my rope around. Yes, I had, in the end figure, figured out a way to get some sleep without falling off. I untied it and secured it around the chimney nearest the collapsed house before tossing the rope down to the wall below. A few of the Shamblers stumbled in through the open doorway and started moaning again. One of them seemed to reach for the rope but then left it alone. Then it stopped moving.

I was only going to get one shot at this.

I was also going to lose the rope.

Nothing for it, though. I had to get away. I walked back to the end of the street, coaxing as many of the Shamblers away from the ruin as I could. When they were in a gathering at the far end, I moved, as quickly as could, back across the roof, thinking the whole time that now would be the moment the tiles gave way and went out from under my feet. But I carried on and took a deep breath as I grabbed the rope.

I swung down and jerked for a moment, my heart thumping. I looked up and saw the chimney stack shifting, almost collapsing. Dust spewed from a fresh crack in the masonry. I had seconds before the thing holding me up collapsed. I lowered myself quickly, palm after palm, until I landed on a small piece of floorboard, jutting out of the wall, and edged along it.

A loud cracking noise from above sent my heart thumping even faster. I'd moved about ten feet along the wooden ledge, about half way to the wall that I need it to reach, when the chimney came crashing through the air behind me, smashing into the floor below. Bricks and rubble shifted beneath me, and I lurched forward. I was going to fall, but instead I used the momentum to run. I slipped and fell forward, grabbing at the wall. I managed to reach it and started climbing, hoping no more of the building would crumble beneath me.

As I lay on top of the wall, breathing heavily, the last remnants of the floorboards collapsed into the building below. Dust spewed upward, filling the ruined building and sweeping out into the street.

When the dust cleared, I was staring down into the faces of a hundred Shamblers outside the house. This spurred me on, and I started to crawl along the top of the wall, pulling myself up where a section was higher and lowering myself carefully down where it was broken. There was one section that had collapsed entirely, leaving a five-foot gap. Clawed hands reached up from below, and I leapt across, praying that the wall on the other side would not give way when I landed.

It didn't. Some of the bricks crumbled and fell beneath me but the wall held firm. Finally, after what seemed like and endless assault course, I was leaning against the far wall. Without a pause I was scrambling up, digging my fingers into cracks and using anything that stuck out as a means to climb up. The drainpipe made most of the climb relatively easy, but I knew I'd burned most of my luck by now, and at any moment the thing could rend from its joints, and I'd go crashing down into the street. Shambler food.

That didn't happen either. Finally, I found myself lying on top of the roof at the other side, panting like a dog after a ten-mile run. Sweat drenched my clothes, and I'd lost my rope, but I'd made it. I looked down into the ruins below where the Shamblers were still stumbling into the building, trying to follow me. They'd gather there and climb over the top of the rubble and each other, but they wouldn't get up the wall.

Time to go.

I crossed five more rooftops and then dropped down onto the platform below. It was only twenty or so feet from the roof, so I didn't hesitate. I had to get down onto it, over the wall, and across the open ground as quickly as I could before the horde could follow me.

:: Record Date 12:07:4787 04:41

So I found myself on the second floor of a building on the other side of the barrier, maybe half a mile away from the open ground. I kept glancing behind me every few seconds, checking the barrier in the distance. Still, none of the Shamblers had breached the top. That was a relief. The last thing I wanted to see was them pouring over the top and following me any further.

By the time I found somewhere to rest the night was coming to an end, and the ambient daylight was getting brighter. I found a place without doors or windows, but it also had no stairway leading up to the upper floor.

I managed to climb the banister attached to the wall up onto the balcony. There, I shut myself in an upstairs room with a boarded-up window. A peephole gap, maybe an inch wide, had been left in one of the boards, so I could keep an eye on the outside, but it wasn't ideal.

If anyone or anything found me in here, I would be trapped, and I'd probably have to punch my way out through the roof.

Right now, I need more sleep. I just hope the Shamblers don't find me again.

:: Record Date 12:07:4787 07:12

A voice woke me.

For a few seconds, I lay there trying to figure out where I was, giving my brain time to catch up. The boarded window, the broken table in the corner, the dusty and torn sofa on which I lay, the smell of mould and of something else more disgusting – I recognised none of these things. I thought I was in a dream and that the voice was something only in my mind. But as the room came into focus, the image of my surroundings more vivid, I remembered the events of the day before.

Plus, the voice didn't go away.

Whoever it was had to be just outside.

I grabbed my rifle and was about to leap from the sofa when it occurred to me that it would make a lot of noise. Instead, I slowly inched my way off the sofa into a crouching position, my feet only just touching the floorboards, and used my spare hand to push myself up into a standing position. A slight creak underfoot – that was the only sound, and it was not very loud.

The problem was the ten feet across creaky floorboards to the boarded-up window. I contemplated just standing still and listening, but I couldn't make out the words. I needed to see who they were, these people. One step at a time, I made my way across the boards, carefully shifting my weight onto my back leg and slowly forward onto the next step. The boards let out tiny creaks of complaint as they bore my weight, but they were not so loud that I thought anyone would hear the - not unless they were very close by.

The voices were faint enough now that I figured they must be twenty, maybe thirty feet from the building and moving away. The last step was a relief, and I leaned forward, peering through the small hole in one of the planks.

Across the street was the open front of what must have been a shop at one point. The door still hung from its hinges, and the space where window panels had once been opened into darkness. It was then that I saw the movement. Three figures moved past the edge of the building before disappearing around the corner. A fourth and fifth emerged, following the first trio. One of them was looking at the ground and then stopped to look up and down the intersecting street. Not one of them looked in my direction.

The second figure crouched to touch the ground. I could see that they were holding a rifle of some sort, but it was so dull and dark outside that I could barely make out the details. The one kneeling muttered something, in a muffled voice that I couldn't hear clearly, and then stood. They continued onward, following the first trio.

It wasn't the one following tracks in the road that had really caught my eye, though. It was the second figure. Like I said, it was dark outside, but there was a certain amount of light to see by, and I noticed that the other person was carrying a rucksack on their back. When they turned away to leave I saw aa slight flash of blue – the colour my stolen pack had been.

They disappeared around the corner, and as they did so, they passed through a ray of light from somewhere, and the colour blue was even more obvious. Whoever had robbed me was outside and had just passed by. That could not be a coincidence, I thought.

To find my hiding place in the library, and rob my spare supplies, and then to pass by the exact building I was hiding in after fleeing half way across the city? No. This wasn't a coincidence.

They were tracking me, and for some reason they'd missed that my tracks ended below in the street. Maybe they'd seen that and were moving off and out of sight deliberately, but they hadn't glanced up at any of the buildings. Confused, puzzled, and unable to decide upon the best course of action, and with only one way out of the building – which meant dropping to the ground and going out the front door again, onto the street where they would see me – I decided to just sit there for a while. I would wait until they had gone.

Other buildings around offered no better options for hiding away, though a few of them have doors that could be shut. I'd already checked several, and there were few with even stable upper floors to hide in.

I had to decide when to make a break for it. They'd gone north, along the very street I needed to take, but that didn't mean I could no longer go that way. I'd just have to do so indirectly. I could get down to the ground floor, sneak along a few streets, and then be on my way.

But did I go now, in a hurry? I'd potentially draw their attention. But If I gave them too much time they would realise they had lost my tracks.

I couldn't wait.

At best, I had only a few minutes before they would be back. I grabbed my stuff and headed out the room into the hallway. I'd have to drop down to the ground level, since the stairs were broken, but something made me stop and listen. Call it gut instinct, or whatever, but something made me pause.

I took a step away from the edge and backed into the doorway just as a wave of dizziness hit me. It only lasted a second or two, but the world swam for those few moments, dark colours washing over my vision as the world swayed. Then it was clear again, and the dizziness faded, but it was followed by a noise below and outside, all around me.

Puzzled, I look down to the ground floor, just ten feet in the distance, straight into the eyes of a Shambler. And not just one. Three more of them were stumbling about below. They'd not been there. I hadn't heard them arrive. Was it this weird shifting thing again?

I went back into the room, less cautious of making noise. If the people who had passed by with listening they'd hear the Shamblers well before they heard me. I got to the boarded-up window and glanced through to see broad daylight outside.

It had been dark before and now it was light, and not just quickly. It had happened instantly. Bright daylight was shining down on the streets, though it was tinted with that strange sepia colour once more, as though a dust storm were sweeping across the skies. This reminded me of the day I arrived here – the strange colour of the light.

There were hundreds of Shamblers outside on the street.

I rubbed my eyes, looked away, and then looked back. I had to be seeing things. Where had they come from?

This still made no sense. I rubbed my eyes again and then, for a second time, the dizziness hit me. The wailing sounds from below vanished with sharp pop of my ears. I held onto the window ledge for a moment, waiting for the nausea to pass, before I looked outside once more.

The bright sepia sky was gone again, and so were the Shamblers. The street outside was empty and dark.

I was still standing there, looking out of the window twenty minutes later, trying to figure out what the hell was going on when the coin dropped.

My idea about phasing had to be true. There was no way both places could exist in the same space. The Shamblers out on the street would have been following the group that passed by minutes before, surely?

One possibility that came to mind was that this place, this city, is shifting, somehow. It's one place but two places, at the same time – or at different times.

Another was that time itself was messed up here. Were there really two versions, both playing out alongside each other, like alternate dimensions? It wasn't something I'd ever experienced or even read about. Sure, the resistance had advanced technology, and had discovered secrets that unearthed the possibility of travel from one place to another through portals – and they could even create those portals – but that was always from one solid and existing place to another.

Both had to be stable to allow it to happen.

The idea of alternate places existing in the same space… Well, *that* was new, as far as I could remember. I do remember that JH experienced some very strange phenomena in The Corridor but not dual existences.

There were so many questions. Places like The Corridor and The Ways defied most laws of reality, that was apparent. The Ways was supposedly endless, like the known universe, and it had never been totally mapped by anyone.

That thought rang a bell. Someone had tried to, I think. A Stygian, maybe? I'd have to find the passage in JH's diary. Yes, they had searched for decades, even hundreds of years, thousands upon thousands of miles, and still they had died not finding an end in any direction.

If a place like that can exist, in all its weirdness, then surely this idea of two places in one could be feasible. It would explain so much – the rapid change in weather and light, the appearance and disappearance of the Shamblers.

It was as I was making these realisations that I caught a glimpse of movement down on the street, past the old shop. Two figures quickly ran across the gap and crouched down by a wall. I clutched my rifle and backed away from the window, quickly moving through the room and into the hall.

"We know you're up there," came a voice from below. "and we know you're armed, but we are too. Chuck your gear down and we'll let you go. I'll give you a minute to consider and then we start firing."

The wave of dizziness came once more, and I'm pretty sure whoever it was outside that had warned me to throw my stuff down was in the middle of speaking again when it hit me. I leaned against the wall, looked over to the window, felt the popping of my ears once more.

This time I saw it happen.

I actually watched the shift.

I don't know how it works, but I can't deny what I witnessed. The light outside, cast through gaps in windows or holes in walls, shifted from darkness to the sepia daylight in less than a second. The whole room blurred. The quietness in the darker place was instantly – with that same popping noise – changed to a rumbling murmur that oddly seemed out of focus or out of tune. Over two or three seconds that sound became clearer – the moans and yells of the Shamblers.

Those were the most prominent changes. The rest were subtle differences between one place and the other, like the position of one of the planks that boarded a window or the place where a broken bottle lay.

So, anyway. The outside erupted once more with the moans of the Shamblers. I stumbled back to the gap below to look down and shook my head. There were four of them now, all looking up at me, arms outstretched, bony clawed hands reaching for me. Ironic, really. The hopelessness of the situation hit me. Not only was I trapped in this room, but I was trapped in two different versions of the room. Be it separated by time or possibly dimension, it mattered little in either version of my reality.

I was blocked by Shamblers, possibly hundreds of them, though I think only a few had noticed my presence.

There was a choice. I still had my guns, I still had the ability to kill, but which reality did I take?

It wasn't a difficult decision at all.

Shamblers can be dangerous in their hundreds, but they aren't armed with weapons.

I lifted the rifle, aimed, and fired a dozen quick shots, one after the other, dropping the Shamblers below me in the hall. I glanced back into the small room, checking I'd let left nothing behind. I had to be fast – I had to be out of here before the shift happened again – or my hasty plan wouldn't work.

I pointed the rifle upwards and reached down, grabbing a piece of masonry. I dropped through, plunging the ten feet onto the ground below. I landed heavily but bent my knees and managed to stay upright without winding myself.

I lowered the rifle and took out three more Shamblers that were closing in. One got too close, reaching for me as I turned to fire, but I took two steps back towards the wall, aimed, and dropped the last.

Without a pause, I ran for the doorway, out into the street, rifle up and aiming as I took every step as quickly as I could, firing at close range as I went. There weren't as many Shamblers in the street as I'd initially thought, but there were still hundreds of them. Thankfully, they weren't crowded together around the shop and most stumbled around aimlessly, but the streets were filled with them in all four directions from the crossroads, as far as I could see.

Trying to stay calm, I picked my direction quickly, judging where my assailants were in the other reality, and decided to turn right and take a side road. I jogged, dropping Shamblers one at a time, and eventually got to the junction of the next street. I turned left, heading north once more.

This street was more sparsely occupied by Shamblers, but those that were there were heading in my direction, and I knew the main mass of them was behind me. I sped up my pace, still only shooting the ones that got too close, and I was half way along the street when I broke free of the creatures

It was then that I took off as fast as I could, stretching legs that were still aching and stiff from sleep, forcing myself onwards – to sprint as fast as I could, away.

And it was only just in time, because I felt the wave of dizziness coming back and had to slow to a stop. I turned around to look back along the street at the hundreds of Shamblers now behind me. There was a good fifty feet between me and the nearest, so I had plenty of room. They wouldn't reach me during the phase.

There was the flash of light as it changed to a dull day where the buildings cast gloomy shadows and the sky was muffled with fog. There was a pop in my ears and the world went quiet once more. I darted to the side of the street and hid behind a wall, listening.

Gunfire erupted back along the street. I guess my minute was up, but I grinned for the first time in days. They would get such a shock when they finally stopped firing long enough to send someone up, only to discover that the room above – where they believe me to be trapped and now dead – was completely empty.

I turned and was about to take off as quickly as I could, but then stopped a few yards later. Something popped into my mind, a curious theory that I had to find an answer to. If these were different dimensions entirely, then my presence, my passage through both, couldn't happen at the same time. It should only take place in one or the other. I looked down at the ground and realised that right there was my answer, well, almost.

I jogged back to where I had stopped as the dizzy wave hit me. There were no Shamblers on the street, that much was clear, so that was part of my answer, but this street was thick with debris and mud and dirt, and the group who had been following me must have had a way to track me. The only thing I could think of was the footprints I would leave in the dirt. I moved further back along the street, my rifle still raised in case one of them turned up. This was risky; they could arrive soon.

But there on the ground was my answer – there were the boot-prints, two of them, where I'd placed my feet apart to brace myself for the dizziness, and there were more prints where I started to run, but behind that, I could not see a single print or churning of the ground.

There were no tracks here to follow when I was in the dimension where the Shamblers roamed.

I turned back along the road, not wanting to wait any longer in case the group turned up, the answer swirling around in my mind. I was thinking of advantages and disadvantages that this could offer. I was about to run when—

"That's far enough," said a voice to my left. I turned and heard a click. I knew I couldn't raise my gun fast enough and saw from the shadows in a doorway just ten yards away, the barrel of a shotgun pointing at me.

"Well," said the voice. "Don't be thinking of shootin' that thing. I'm faster than you think. Don't make me do this."

I lowered the weapon and raised the other hand.

"I don't want any trouble," I said. "I just want to leave."

"Really." His reply was flat and not really a question. The man stepped from the shadows. I'd been expecting a younger man, maybe somebody even my age, but his dark hair and beard was mottled with grey. He wore a hat that reminded me of some of the cowboy comics I'd read when I was younger – the ones my mother had given me – and he also wore a long coat – a duster! that's what it's called – just like the cowboys did.

"Now where you after in such a hurry"?

I glance back down the road and could see movement in the far distance. Whether this man was with the others or not, I'd soon find out, because they must have caught my trail and were now following me again.

"Don't worry about them," said the man. "It's obvious, now I've got a good look at you, that you're not one of them pale-skin Stygians." said the man. "Now, if you can sling that rifle over your shoulder and just put out your hands, I'll lower this shotgun. I know you're not one of them, but I don't know if you mean trouble."

"I don't," I said, slinging the rifle over my shoulder by the strap and holding my hands out with palms facing him. "I didn't intend to even be here this long."

He nodded. "You seem to be heading somewhere in a hurry."

I heard footsteps down coming from down the street and saw some of the figures that had cornered me in the building, running towards us.

"They're with me," he said.

"That was my worry," I said.

He frowned at this. "We don't mean you any harm. You're one of us."

"What do you mean?" I asked.

"Meaning that you are human," he said. "We got no gripe with our own kind. Where are you from? Not here, from the way you are dressed."

I look down at what had been once been a uniform. It was bedraggled now. My jacket was dirty and worn, and the trousers would have been better off just burned.

"I travelled here from elsewhere."

"That much I guessed, which makes me very curious," said the man. The three figures running up the street slowed down, weapons drawn. The one in front was a tall man with long dark hair, and he looked angry at first, but then his expression became puzzled.

"I think we made ourselves a bit of a mistake here," said the man still standing with his shotgun pointing at me. "This fella isn't a Stygian."

"Obviously not," said the tall man. He holstered the gun he'd been carrying. The two people behind him, a young woman and another man, maybe a few years younger than the woman, lowered their spears. I found it strange that some were armed with what I considered higher tech weapons and yet the others carried primitive ones.

"How did you get out of that building back there?" asked the man with the long dark hair.

How did I describe what was happening? It wasn't as though I had control over it.

"I have a way of getting around places," I said, but it sounded lame the moment came out of my mouth.

"You can get around places? Really," said the man. "That the best you can do? We had that place covered, and that room has only one way out of it, and yet here you are, a street away."

"You wouldn't understand if I tried to explain it to you," I said. "I don't really know why it's happening myself. It's only since I arrived in this place."

"You arrived?" asked the long-haired man.

"Like I said," said the man with the shotgun. "Not from here. No, not many left, these days. What's left of us is so low in number that I'm pretty sure I'd recognise him if he was."

"Are you people from the exiles?" I asked.

"What do you know of that?" asked the long-haired man.

"That's a long, long story," I said. "But I've heard that

this place was split, at one point. The exiles and…I don't know the name of the others."

"Did you get past the gate and come back this way?" asked the woman.

"No," I said. "I came through another doorway that leads here, and it's only one-way," I said. "I can't go back."

"The one in the alley?"

"Yes," I said, surprised that they knew about it.

The man with the shotgun nodded at the long-haired man. "Where they all arrive," he said.

"Wait a minute," I said. "You said gateway? Do you know where the gate out of here is?"

"Of course," said the long-haired man. "There's only two. The one in the alley, where the Stygians come from, and the one in the fortress to the north."

I nodded. "I'd hoped as much. Look, I don't want any trouble. I just wanted to find the gate and get out of here."

"What's your name, anyway?" asked the man with the shotgun.

"Connor," I said, thinking of no reason to lie. "Connor."

"That's the name. The one she is looking for," said the girl behind them. "The ghost lady."

"Ilya?" asked. "You've met her?"

The woman nodded. Well at least there was some good news. Ilya was still around. I just needed to find her.

"I met her a few days ago," said the woman. "She asked after someone by the name of Connor, but I didn't know anyone by that name."

"The ghost girl is a friend of yours?" asked the man with the long dark hair.

I nodded. "We came here together but were separated."

"This gets more interesting by the minute," he said. "She's been looking for you and making our lives a pain, if I may say," he said. "Difficult to get rid of someone who ain't really there."

"Do you know where she is now?" I asked.

"Sure, we do," he said. "She's back at our camp, refusing to leave unless we help find you. No, I'm not telling you where that is. Not unless you start talking. Where you come from, if you know much about the Stygians, and that thing you did. How is it you're in one place one minute then another place?"

"Look, like I said. I don't know why it's happening. One moment I feel dizzy, and then all this…changes." I waved my hand, meaning everything. "It seems that I shift from one place to the other, and it's the same as this place but different enough. The other place is full of Shamblers, and the sky is a bright yellow colour. It warmer there, as well. I don't understand it any better than that. I don't know if it's another plane of existence, or another version of this place, or even a different time. It doesn't make sense to me. I can't explain it to myself, let alone explain it so you understand."

"Keep going," he said.

"When I was up in the building that you surrounded, I shifted. I fought my way through the Shamblers and out and headed along this street. I shifted back again about a hundred yards up the road. Go look for yourself, you'll see the tracks start halfway down the street."

"We already spotted that," said the woman.

"So, while you were aiming weapons at the building you thought I was in, I was running past you, except I wasn't in the same place as you, even though it looks almost the same. I phased back again up the street and got stopped by your friend here before I could get out of here."

"That's why I thought you came out of nowhere," said the man with the shotgun. "You snuck up on me pretty good."

"Sorry," I said. "I didn't mean to. I don't mean any of this, but you guys, you did rob me, didn't you? At the library? Was that you? You took my stuff."

"We didn't rob anyone," said the woman. "I found the stuff there and we take what we find to get by. Didn't see anyone around until you came back after we had searched the place."

"There was a rucksack in the library. I'd been camping there a few nights there," I said.

"You can have it back, minus some of the food," said the man with the dark hair. "Already ate some of it." He shrugged. "Didn't think it's owner was still around. We were surprised to find something up there and presumed that somebody had been and gone."

"I said it seemed odd, that we might be stealing, when we found it," said the woman.

"There was no evidence," said the dark-haired man. "We couldn't find anybody. I just presumed that whoever owned it was dead already."

"What is it you want with that gate?" asked the man with the shotgun.

"I want to go through it," I said. "I'm trying to trace my mother, though it's been a long time since she would have come through here. If she came through here.

"Your mother?"

"Eleanor Halldon," I said.

"Say who?" asked the man with the shotgun. He looked surprised. "Did you say Eleanor?"

"Yes."

"She is your mother?"

I noticed that they all looked shocked now.

"What?" I asked.

"I didn't know she had a kid," said the man with the dark hair.

My heart jumped at this.

"You know her?"

"Yes. Don't worry, as far as I know, she ain't dead. She was the one that led us against the Stygians years ago, when most of us got out."

"She was here? How long ago?"

"Oh, I don't know," said the man with the shotgun. "About ten years since they went. She was here about five years, and gradually gathered the different groups into one, stopped all the feuding."

"And you're sure it was her?" I asked. At last, a clue.

"Eleanor Halldon," he said. "She arrived through same way you did, in that alleyway. It's how we know about the Ashlands gate, which is where we've been try to get through the last ten years or so."

"Where is she now?" I asked.

"She went through the portal. She made it and took a lot of other folk with her on the night we attacked the Stygian fort. Some of us got pushed back by reinforcements and didn't make it through the gate. Ever since then, there's not been enough of us. There were four maybe five hundred of us back then, and we stormed the place, but when the last of us were trying to get through the gate, more of those damn Stygians appeared and pushed us back into the ruins. That's where we've been ever since."

The woman took over. "She came here when I was very young, looking for somebody as well. Her father and mother and her family. But, of course, this place was a nightmare. Feuding gangs, Stygian patrols, dead things walking around. I remember how she banded the clans together."

"It took us a good few years," said the man with the shotgun. "Getting the gear together, training folks to fight together. Because no one group wanted to follow another, and they all seemed to end up trusting Eleanor, your mother ended up leading us after she caused the damn revolt against that idiot that used to push everybody around."

"I need to get through that portal," I said.

"You and us both," said the man with the shotgun. "And I have some ideas brewing. Maybe between you and that ghost girl, we may have a chance. If you're willing to work with us and help."

"Anything," I said.

"That fort," he continued. "The place is pretty tight, and there's too many of them for us to fight. We would try to take them down, but we only have the two guns, and they are all heavily armoured. They get reinforcements from somewhere. Every now and then, a whole bunch of them arrive through that alleyway. There's only a couple of dozen of us left – not enough to take on what they've got – but if somebody who could sneak around, like you can, were to help, maybe we could cause enough trouble that we can find a weakness. If you can convince that ghost friend of yours to help."

"I'm sure she will," I said.

"If you say so. She's been pretty uncooperative so far, and she's been insisting that unless we find you, she's not helping us at all. So, we've been searching the city for the last few days to find you. Course, we didn't know it was you we'd found. We didn't mean to scare you away."

"You fired on me," I said.

"Ah, yeah. That was just to get you to submit. We weren't actually aiming at you. Of course, then we found the place empty, that was quite the surprise."

"To me too, most of the time," I said.

"Look," said the man with the long dark hair. "How about we start from scratch. Forget all that happened. We'll get your stuff back, you can come to the camp, and we can start talking and planning."

"Sounds good to me," I said. "Are we close to the fort now?"

"Dangerously close," said the woman. "Like, three streets away. We should get going. There could be a patrol at any time, and trust me, you won't want to meet one. They're heavily armed, and they don't like talking to people."

:: Record Date 12:07:4787 11:49

Ilya, it seemed, was more relieved to see me than I thought she would be. I'd thought that after her experience in The Corridor, and the realisation that she was kind of dead – and maybe blamed me – it would have soured any chance of us being friends, but it hadn't. She rushed over to me, when I walked into the camp, and tried to hug me, which was a little embarrassing since she can't touch anything. But I grinned, feeling happier for the first time in a long while. I'd found her, and I had news of my mother, my first lead in a while. I just had to get past a fort of heavily armed Stygians.

She also had a lot to tell me. Apparently while I'd fled from the mass of Shamblers that had been there when I arrived, she had appeared in the same spot, but there weren't any Shamblers. She had been alone. Of course, it made sense. We'd arrived at the same time, in the same place, but I was phased into the place where the Shamblers were and she wasn't.

Then she bumped into the exiles on the third day. She was welcomed with a barrage of shots. Then, not really knowing who or what she was but realising that she wasn't a Stygian weapon, they soon calmed down and started to talk.

The Stygians, it seemed, had quite a fortress over near where the gate must be, built from scrap and old buildings, and they'd blocked off a lot of the streets. There were searchlights covering the roads all around, so it was difficult for anyone to get close, let alone get in.

"These people need to get in," she said. "They asked me to go and look, because it seems I can't be harmed by anything, but I don't know. I didn't want to go anywhere near the gate without finding you first, in case I ended up forced to go through it. Then we'd be completely separated, and you may lose any chance you have of going through.

"It appears that we're both drafted to help them escape," she continued. "It's what we want, anyway. Can't be much of a life being trapped here. I've seen how they live. They grow what food they can, but they have to try and hide it across the city, and Stygian patrols have raided places in the past. They haven't found this place, and a few of the other hideaways, but they have lost a few people to the raids over the last decade. Thankfully the Stygians haven't raided for a few years."

This place, as she called it, turned out to be one of the old factories I'd seen in the distance, on the other side of the city. It looked derelict from the outside, and the exiles had done well to maintain that appearance. Even if you walked around the inside of the main building you'd hardly know it was occupied. They live underground, several floors below the old factory and the power plant next to it, and the entrance to the hideaway is a few streets away, in a ruined building rather than inside the factory.

Two dozen of them live there - mostly men and women in their twenties, as well as a couple of children who must have been born in this place, since the others managed to escape, because they're young enough that they can't have known anywhere else.

They also have a cat called Henry, who seems to have taken to Ilya and tries to rub against her leg and then looks puzzled when it doesn't work. It's quite comical to watch his frustration, but it doesn't seem to put him off. He doesn't seem to want to leave her alone.

Thankfully, I got my kit back from them, minus most of the food. However, pretty much everything else was still in the rucksack. The guy who gave it to me seemed reluctant to hand it over. I don't suppose they get many good finds like a rucksack full of equipment.

I slept in a bunk for what must have been ten hours, and even after that I still felt exhausted. When I woke I was taken to a large hall they use as a mess hall, which to me looks like it was originally a large storeroom of some sort. I sat down opposite the two older men that I'd met near the fort, and Ilya perched on the edge of the sofa nearby.

"So," said the man with the long dark hair – Jonson was

his name. They introduced me to everyone the night before, but I was unlikely to remember all the names. "We've been talking, trying to come up with ideas. We're keen to get you, and Ilya, here, out there if we can persuade you. We're hoping that you can use your unique abilities to get a look around the place, maybe see if there's a way to cause a distraction long enough for us to launch an attack."

"Just us?" asked Ilya.

"No," said Bronn. Bronn was the oldest in the colony and was the man who'd stopped me on the street with his shotgun pointing at me. "We'll be there as well, some of us. Just case you need help. We're hoping Ilya here could just walk in and sneak around a bit, and if you happen to shift while you're there, maybe you can go too."

"Doesn't seem like much of a plan," said Ilya.

"No," said Bronn. "Not at the moment. We're short on ideas of how to launch an attack when we're heavily outgunned. We don't think there are that many in there, but they have the weapons. They also have two heavy cannons, up on the front wall of the building, that could devastate anything coming too close."

"Sounds dangerous," I said.

Bronn nodded. "I'm not going to wash over how much we're asking of you, here. I know you could be tempted to just go in and sneak through the portal, so I'm being honest and asking you to help us. Not for me, but for these kids.

Yeah, most have grown up now, but they were kids when they lost their families, who managed to escape. We need to get them back to their folks, and I think you are our best chance yet."

"So just go in, sneak around, see what we can find?" asked Ilya.

"For now, yes," said Bronn. "We figure if we can get some idea of the layout, we may be able figure out a plan to attack it."

"We've really never been able to get close enough to find any existing weak points," said Jonson. "We've got the disadvantage of them being heavily armed."

"When you say heavily armed, what do you mean?"

"They use weapons like we've not seen before. They burn, cut you to shreds."

"Shredders, like this," I said holding up my rifle.

"No, these guns are bigger than that,"

"Trust me," I said. "This does the same sort of damage, and so do my handguns. They're pulse weapons that use a surge of electromagnetic power to tear things apart. They run on batteries."

Jonson shook his head. "We don't have anything other just a couple of shotguns and a few rifles, and not much ammunition – a few hundred rounds, at most. That's where the problem lies."

"They've got the firepower," said Bron. "We would run out in seconds."

"I can do it," said Ilya. "Those weapons don't touch me."

"I'm in," I said. As much as I needed to get through the portal, I couldn't ignore these people. They were my mother's friends, and they were stuck here.

"Are you sure?" asked Bron. "We're aware we are asking you to risk your lives."

We both nodded.

"Okay," said Jonson. "Glad you're on board. Now, we know when they're most active, these Stygians. They stay in their fort in the day and run patrols at night, so during daylight the base tends to go quiet, and they even leave the two cannons unmanned. My suggestion is you two, and a few of us, go take up hiding places nearby and wait for a good time to sneak in. Then Ilya goes in, looks around – just looking for any weaknesses or areas of the base that are empty that we may be able to break through to. Then you get out. If it's possible for us to make a hole in that wall and sneak our way through to the portal, that's what we'd like to do. A full-on attack could mean heavy losses. I don't want o to lose anyone."

"And me?" I asked.

"Likewise, if you phase while were there. Otherwise it will be too dangerous for you to get in. We don't even know what you'll be able to see when you get in there. For the start, this is just a recon mission. Then we can see what we can plan. We've been ten years trying to figure this out, so we're not hurrying to die over it."

"Okay, well, no time like now," said Ilya.

The rest of us just looked at her, surprised at her enthusiasm.

:: Record Date 13:07:4787 13:27

"Your mother is a good woman," Bronn said as we walked. It had taken us the best part of the day to get to the Stygian base, and we had been walking for maybe three hours in silence before he first spoke. Ilya had taken to walking ahead of us, with three of the other exiles and Jonson, and eventually I could only just make her out in the distance. It was probably close to midday when he first spoke.

"Did you know her well?" I asked.

"Fairly," he said. "She was a good friend and saved my life a number of times." He was quiet for a moment. "She helped a lot of us with her skills."

"Skills?" I asked.

"She was a fighter," he said. "And her knowledge of tech was damn good, but she was a doctor, as well. I've got a scar." He pointed to his side. "Right here, where one of those Stygians took a shot at me. Didn't think I was gonna make it, but she managed to stitch me up anyway. She had a little bottle of stuff that she could inject into you, like some miracle drug. She kept it hidden and only dished it out sparingly. It was only a small bottle, but I got a bit of it that day. I think the bottle was empty by the time she led everybody through the gate."

"Why weren't you with them?" I asked.

"There weren't just the older folk, and the scavengers, to think of, back then," he said. "There were the kids. Most of these still here would have been under six years old, back then. When your ma led us to attack the base, I was one of the ones who drew a straw to watch the kids at a safe house not far from the fort. We were meant to just keep them safe and be ready for when we could take the kids through. Unfortunately, that didn't happen for us. I'm sure she would have come back if she could have done."

"So, you got stuck here?"

"The portal is one-way, chief," he said. "Just one-way, like the other. And a lot of the groups got through, but we had the kids and elderly split into three groups in various locations. We were about a half-mile from the battle, ready to go when the time was right, but then when the call went up and we got moving, another group of Stygians had been missed, somehow. They killed one of our patrols and cut us off, and we couldn't get word to the main force. I'd imagine your mother led folks through their thinking all the Stygians were dead, but of course there was this other patrol, probably a reinforcement group that hadn't been noticed. They kept us stuck in a building just a few hundred yards from the portal, for about two days, and then more and more of them turned up.

"We found a sewer entrance and got out, but we were miles away from the fort, and the Stygians took it over again before we could get there. My brother, Jono, died holding off the patrol while we got the kids into the sewer."

"I'm sorry to hear that," I said.

"Don't be. He died protecting those he cared about. Best we can do, really. Anyway, that's where we are. We're the ones that got left behind, through no fault of your ma's. She had over five hundred people to get through that portal. That only twenty or so didn't make it was a pretty good score, far as we're concerned. We just been trying to get through to catch up with them for so long now."

"Then we need to make sure you do," I said.

He nodded, and we continued walking in silence.

That was the last we spoke before we got to the Stygian base.

:: Record Date 13:07:4787 20:09

They may have built quite a fortress to defend the streets leading up to the portal, but there was still plenty of places that I could get to not far from the wall that gave me a good view of the fort. The building I chose must've been another factory, and it had a water tower, and although some of the ladder spokes were broken, I managed to climb up and crawl across the flat surface at the top. There was a hole in some of the brickwork, and I could clearly make out most of the outside of the fort and the tops of the buildings.

I'm surprised they hadn't flattened the building. It wasn't high enough that I could see inside the fort, so I couldn't make out the individual buildings or doors, and I could only follow the movements of those on the outer wall, but for a sniper, wanting to take out targets on the wall, it was still the ideal spot.

The compound itself is was probably only a few hundred yards across in each direction, and it was another quarter mile from there to the city wall, so we had every direction around the fort to consider. We moved into place late in the evening and took up watch positions. We didn't have radios, so we had to make our plans in advance and know when to leave.

We stayed hidden for most of the night, and as daylight came, I watched as the last patrol of Stygians enter the fort through the main gate. I noticed the two cannons on the top of the wall, perched on either side of the gate, but they were unmanned and had been since we arrived. The Stygians didn't feel threatened out here, it seemed.

As planned, half an hour after the last patrol had entered the fort, Ilya appeared from one of the side streets where she had been hiding. She moved quickly along the street and stopped at the corner, peering across the open ground at the fort. It was a good hundred yards of flat ground with no cover, and although I could see that there was no one on the wall, I wondered if she could.

Then she was moving, running across the dirt and rubble strewn ground. She stopped when she reached the wall, turned around, and looked up at the tower where I was hiding. She gave a quick wave and then she was gone, walking straight through the wall.

All went quiet.

"I wonder if she's found anything interesting," I said to Bron. He'd joined me a few minutes after Ilya went into the compound and we lay there for twenty minutes before we spoke.

"No idea. She's been gone a long time. You don't think they could have a way of capturing her?" I asked.

"I don't know," he said. "I wouldn't think so. I think someone in her state is pretty much untouchable, but unfortunately that goes the same the other way around."

"True."

"She can't really do anything besides go and look," he said.

It was then, almost in reply to his comment, that the massive gate at the front of the compound swung quickly open.

I frowned. "You were saying…" I said.

Bronn crouched down to peer through the same gap as me. "The hell is going on?"

Then the Stygians appeared, pushing quickly through the gate, a dozen of them, half of them turning one way and the other half going the other. Most weren't wearing armour, but they had weapons. We watched, puzzled, as they hurried around the outside of the fort wall and disappeared from view.

Then more came, moving to their left and following the others.

"Er…how many of them are in there?"

"About that many plus a few more," said Bronn. "Not many more, though. The hell is going on?"

Then the gunfire started, and the streets the other side of the fort lit up with shredder blasts.

I'd never seen a Stygian before and had only heard the tales and read the descriptions in JH's journals. They only ever mentioned Nua'lath and D'hamir and Sha'ris, so my reference was limited. These figures were taller than men by maybe a foot, and they were much thinner, their skin very pale, almost translucent, and they moved fast.

"She must've churned up the hornet's nest," Bronn said. "Look, that way." he pointed across the fort toward the buildings the other side. I looked that way but only saw the Stygians in the street on the other side of the fort, and nothing else, until I spotted her. It had to be her, running along the street quite a distance ahead of the Stygians, who were firing a blaze of shots after her. Ilya.

"This wasn't what I had planned," Bronn said, seeming unsure of what to do.

The Stygians may have been faster than most men, but Ilya was faster still, keeping them trailing after her, firing into the buildings as they tried to hit her.

I looked down at the front of the fort. The gate was still wide open. Not a Stygian in sight.

"Erm…I don't know how many are in there, but the gates are open, and there's now two dozen less of them. How many do you reckon that leaves?"

Bronn looked down at the gate, then back at me. "Not too many."

I gripped the shredder rifle tightly. "No time like now," I said, repeating Ilya's words. I also reached to my waist and held out one of my handguns. "Trust me. This will hurt them a lot more than your shotgun. At least at a distance. It also never runs out."

"There's just two of us," said Bronn, but I could see something in his eyes – excitement. He took the handgun and thrust it into his belt. "I can't signal the others."

"Then it's just us. Just aim and pull the trigger," I said. "And don't worry about anything else. Think you're ready?"

"No, but let's do it. We have to."

We hurried from the top of the tower, down the ladder and out of the building, pausing only to check the street outside in case there was a stray Stygian wandering around, but there wasn't.

"This is crazy," Bronn said as we prepared to run for the gate.

"You don't have to come if you don't want to," I said and started running.

"What? You're joking. The chance to kill some of them?" he shouted as he caught up with me.

Then I was running, and I could hear Bronn running just behind me. I hurried, pushing myself as fast as I could toward the main gate which still lay wide open. I reached the opening, slowed down, and crouched low, peering inside. It seemed deserted. I crept through the gap and made for the nearest cover. Twenty yards away was a stack of crates, and another twenty yards beyond that was the first of the buildings. I ran, with Bronn close behind me. We reached the stack of crates without a problem and stopped to catch our breath.

"The main building first," I said, looking around. There were three houses in a row along the eastern side of the compound, a large warehouse building in the centre with a door at either end, and some ruined buildings around it. Beyond that was an alleyway that led into what looked like a courtyard that twenty or more houses faced onto, all surrounding an area of trees and grass.

That was where the portal would be, I thought.

We moved again, hurrying towards the warehouse, just as the door on the left opened and a Stygian stepped out. I already had my gun raised, ready, and dropped to one knee, firing. I missed the first shot but hit with the two that followed. The Stygian fell, dropping his rifle, but another figure stepped through the door, this one firing blindly. I dived to the ground and fired another trio of shots, but the Stygian backed into the building and the shots hit the wall with a loud crack.

When the Stygian peered out again, firing blindly once more, Bronn was ready. A single shot and the Stygian dropped to the ground. We ran for the door.

"Damn, this thing is like a toy," he said.

"You want to try one of those rifles," I said as I passed the body of the first Stygian, his rifle lying on the ground a few feet from him.

I reached the door to the warehouse just as shots rang out from the other side of the fort. I turned and pushed my back against the corrugated wall. Several figures moved outside the line of three houses and started running across the dirt ground towards us, raining shots at us.

"Inside," I shouted, pulling open the door.

Bronn went in ahead of me, but only by a second or two, and we found ourselves face to face with three more of the enemy. We had surprised them, though, and they didn't have weapons in their hands. Two of them fell to my shots before Bronn could shoot the last with a glancing blow to the shoulder that knocked him to the ground. The Stygian rolled away behind a stack of boxes and came up on the other side with a hand gun, already firing. He had barely made it to his feet when Bronn dropped him with another well-aimed shot.

"I'm getting used to this this thing," he said.

We quickly took cover and scanned around for more of the enemy. The distant gunfire from outside had ceased, and I knew the Stygians that had chased Ilya would be back soon.

"Quickly, over here," Bronn said. I turned to find him crouched behind a large metal container that would give cover but still allow us to see both doors. I ran and skidded around the back of it just in time as the Stygians burst through both doors. Two came through the left entrance and three from the right.

"I've got the left," Bronn shouted, opening fire and dropping one of the Stygians. I felt something hot pass by my face and blast into the side of the container. I fired a volley in return, sending both groups diving for cover, but then I heard Bronn cry out in pain and spun to see him crouched on the floor holding his leg.

No one could have shot him in the leg from the front.

I spun around just in time to see the Stygian, who had been hidden the whole time, up on the balcony above. I raised my weapon and opened fire before he could aim at me, hitting him in the face. A lucky shot and a fatal one. The creature flew backward and slumped to the floor.

I turned back around, noticing that the Stygians coming in the front doors had taken the opportunity to charge us, but they weren't quick enough, and even as I felt the blasts of their rifles surge by me, I opened fire, but not before I switched my own weapon to full automatic fire. I'd only tried this mode once or twice and knew the gun would overheat very quickly.

A three second blast was all that was needed. The four remaining Stygians dropped to the floor as they ran across the open area in front of me. One sweeping arc and the weapon ploughed all of them down. As I expected, the weapon went into shutdown, a flashing red light blinking on the top to indicate that the trigger was disabled.

"You ok?" I asked Bronn. He was sitting on the ground now, grasping a nasty looking burn on his leg.

"Yeah," he said. "No, not really. This stings like mad, but it's not too bad. Just a glancing shot. Could be worse."

"Stay here," I said. "Don't try to move it. I'll be back."

A quick lap of the circumference of the compound told me that there was no one else left inside. I didn't see any movement from the beyond the archway that led into the area where I suspected the portal to be, and with all the noise we had just made, I expected every Stygian in the fort at the time had rushed to the warehouse.

I walked toward the archway, wary of any other Stygians that may be hidden there. I could see through the arch that there was a clearing with grass and trees. It had to be the park that JH found the portal in. There were at least twenty houses surrounding it, most derelict, each with its own small backyard and a wooden fence with a gate that that opened out onto the green.

I was right. There, in the middle of the park, blazed the portal.

The temptation was almost overwhelming. It was there, right front of me. I could go right now. But no. The same thought my mother must have had when she had been here hit me. She could have probably made it alone, back then, if she'd rushed in shooting, but it would have been just her, and she had no Ilya to cause a distraction.

That would have been at the price of someone else's life. No, instead, she had spent five years helping the remnants of the civilians of this town turn themselves into an army ready to fight their way through.

It was beautiful to see it, though, blazing in the middle

of the grass.

There were no Stygians in any of the houses, but I didn't stay very long in each. Five minutes later, I was back at the warehouse, where I expected Bronn to be, but he was gone. I glanced around, wondering where the hell he was.

"Up here," came the voice. I looked up toward the guard post near the front gate. Somehow, he had climbed up the steps to the walkway that overlooked the outside, near the gate. Bronn was sitting in a swivel seat attached to a rather nasty looking cannon that was now pointed outwards into the city. "Seems I found myself an even bigger one of those guns of yours," he said. "And not a moment too soon, either. They're coming."

I looked toward the cannon at the other side of the gate. This one had a ladder leading up to it; I could climb but Bronn wouldn't have been able to.

"Genius," I said.

"Oh yeah," said Bronn. "They'll have such a surprise when they come back. I couldn't just sit there knowing they was coming soon. This is our chance, boy. Get that gate shut and get up here!"

The gate was easier than I thought it would be, and it swung closed easily as I pulled it. I slammed the crossbar across it, to stop the Stygians pushing it open from the outside, and ran for the ladder. I climbed as quickly as I could and pulled myself up into the seat next to the cannon, looking out over the open ground beyond the gate.

They were in view already, along one of the streets that led straight to the fort. It was nearly dark, and both units had joined together to head back. When I saw them approaching down the main street towards the compound, I thought it couldn't be more perfect.

There was no sign of Ilya. I'm not sure how they could have caught her, but I was still relieved that she wasn't with them.

I glanced over to Bronn. "You gonna be ok?" He was leaning against the side of the outer wall, his leg bent as he sat in the seat, but he wasn't giving up.

"I'm good. Only chance to do this," he said. "We can do it."

I crouched down and he nodded again, crouching behind the wall, grimacing as he knelt half in half out of the seat. I peered over and raised my hand. They approached slowly. Bronn nodded his understanding. I would give the signal, and then we would fire.

There were two dozen of them, all armed. I had to hope that these guns were powerful enough to sweep most of them away before they could return fire. They got to within forty feet of the entrance, and I nodded to Bronn. We both sat up, grasped the controls for the cannons, and fired.

It was over in seconds.

I was impressed by my assault rifle, and I've fired some vehicle-mounted guns before, but I've never fired a weapon as powerful as the cannons guarding the Stygian base. They were shredders, just like most other Resistance weapons, but these were a magnitude larger, and must have been attached to a cylinder underneath with some form of super battery power.

The front of the cannon began to spin as I squeezed the trigger, and for a moment nothing seemed to happen. No flashes of shredder fire leapt from the nozzle – nothing. It just seemed to be winding up. I started to panic. The Stygians would hear the noise of the weapon's revolving barrel and it wouldn't fire quickly enough.

Some of the Stygians looked up at the wall, surprised. We'd been caught. Then the weapon leapt into life. Hundreds and hundreds of shards blazed down onto the enemy below. I pivoted the gun to sweep across them, and the blaze of fire crossed a twin stream as Bronn had the same idea and swept his line of fire towards my side. More than half of the Stygians fell in the first sweep. A few of them turned and tried to run, and another half-dozen tried to rush for the front gate, to get out from under the blaze, but, by some lucky judgement, when I swept my cannon down and across the front of the gate, Bronn swept his outwards to strike the ones that were fleeing.

That was all it took. Thirty seconds later we were sitting in the seats, listening to the cannons wind down until we sat in silence.

Not a single Stygian remained alive on the ground outside. Two dozen of them lay dead. Bronn started bellowing and waving his fist at the dead. "We did it," he shouted, then nearly slipped and fell out of the seat. He managed to steady himself and shook his head. "Almost a bad end, there," he said with a grin. "Maybe you could help me get down out of this thing?"

By the time I managed to help him down to ground level he was sweating, and hot to the touch, but he was still cheerful. I looked at the wound on his leg. It would heal, I knew, but I had none of the medicine that my mother had supposedly carried and wouldn't be able to help him much.

"I can bind the wound," I said, "but not much else."

"I'm good," he said. "But more importantly, we need to get word to the others, tell them to come while we still hold this place."

"Before more Stygians turn up to take it back," I said.

He nodded at this. "We know they change their patrols every few weeks or so, but you never know when one is due. They could arrive today or a week from now. It's not worth waiting."

"I can go," said Ilya. I jumped. She'd walked right through the gate and appeared next to us.

"Gods," said Bronn. "You scared the hell out of me."

"Sorry," she said with a smile. "My plan worked then?"

"Oh yes," Bronn replied. "But, seriously? That was a plan?"

Ilya shook her head. "No, not really. I went in intending to just look around, as we planned before, but as I went into the big building over there, thinking I was sneaking pretty well, I just walked into a bunch of them. They yelled a lot and I ran through the wall. I guess that stirred them up."

Bronn laughed. "Stirred them up good and proper. Now we have a chance. We have to move quickly."

"I'll go. I can get there faster than any of you," said Ilya.

There was a bang on the gate, and I turned to run up the gangway, weapon drawn, but Ilya held up her hand and stepped through, then came back. "It's okay, it's the others. They must have seen what happened."

The other exiles hurried through the gate when I opened it and we helped Bronn toward one of the buildings. Two of them headed out to double check the compound once more, to make sure there were no Stygians left in hiding.

"You sure you're okay to go? I can do it," I said.

"You stay here and guard the place. I can't do that, and I don't need to sleep," Ilya said. "And I don't get tired. How else do you think I managed to run them around half the city for the last hour?"

"True," I said.

"I'll go as quickly as I can. You make sure you hold this place till I can get them here."

I nodded. "Tell them to hurry as though their lives depend on it. Because they do."

Then she was gone, vanishing back through the gate.

:: Record Date 16:07:4787 11:46

A day and a half passed, and I was sitting at one of the cannon positions overlooking the gate, watching out across the streets, when I saw the distant movement. I snapped from my daze. Sitting in one place for so long was more tiring than being active, but after doing two shifts in a row I needed to sleep. The other exiles insisted on taking their turns, but I found that when I lay down to sleep, I just couldn't drift off.

Bronn's wound was healing, but it was painful for him. All we could do was make sure he stayed in the bed that we put him in, which was difficult, since he always wanted to get up. Stubborn old man.

I watched as the distant movement became a crowd of people. At first, I gripped the cannon and hid behind the barrier, trying to make out who was coming. If it was a Stygian patrol, I would have to deal with them, and I didn't want them to see me before it was too late. We'd cleared the bodies from the street, so there was no outward indication that the fort had fallen, and I hoped this ruse would work if needed.

But it wasn't the Stygians. By the time they were a hundred yards away, I could see clearly that it was the exiles – all of them. They were hurrying, jogging along the street, almost like a troop of soldiers in training. By the time they got to the compound, I could see they were utterly exhausted. One of the exiles opened the gates for them and they hurried in, each of them carrying several sacks.

I left another of the exiles up on the cannon to watch for us and went to find Jonson.

"Damn you," he said, before I could speak. "You actually took this place by yourselves?"

I shook my head. "We couldn't have done it without Ilya – she caused such a stir that they were left wide open. We had to take the opportunity. Most of them left the base to chase her, so it was really a clean-up. Bronn is wounded, but it will heal."

"I heard," said Jonson. "Is it a bad wound?"

"Hurts him a lot," I replied.

"Well, we've got stuff to help him," Jonson said. "But if it's bad, I've got something that will fix it quicker."

I followed him into the building where Bronn was resting and watched as he drew out a small vial of liquid and a syringe.

"Where'd you get that?" asked Bronn.

"Elle gave it to me before she went. On the night we were due to leave. She wanted us to have it in case any of the kids were hurt."

"Dammit, that's not meant for me," Bronn said as Jonson injected a small amount of it into his leg.

"It's for anyone that really needs it, and we need you up and moving. We need to get out of here. Right now. This stuff will work its magic in less than an hour. I need you with a weapon in your hand, ready for whatever we find on the other side."

He turned to me. "Have you stripped this place?"

"Oh yes," I said, and we had. While we waited for the exiles to come, we took shifts in hunting through the compound for anything of use. The warehouse was a complete mess after we'd ransacked it.

:: Record Date 16:07:4787 12:38

And so it was that no more than an hour later, I found myself standing next to the portal that led out of Riverfall and into the next stage of my journey. The Ashlands – I hoped.

I didn't know what I would find there, or how much had changed since JH went through, or even since my mother led the exiles out of this place. But I wasn't alone. I started this journey alone, and then I found Ilya. Now I had Bronn, Jonson and the exiles. So not just one, but over two dozen people stood with me as I prepared to take the next step.

I would lead the group through, as I promised I would. I also insisted I would go first, and that they followed me quickly. The exiles were newly armed with Stygian weapons and gear, and they were quite a formidable force, now. In the time they'd had, they'd gathered the stuff that we found and built makeshift trolleys to haul it along. They managed to butcher some of the armour the Stygians wore to make their own, and they did so in minutes.

They were far more resourceful than I had ever been. They even hauled both of the cannons down from the wall, batteries and all, and placed those on another makeshift trolley. The cannons weren't as big as I'd first imagined.

There was a massive amount of supplies in the base that we couldn't take. It was just too much for even two dozen people to carry. But most of what the Stygians considered to be food was not anything that any of us would have risked eating anyway, so it was left untouched.

We stood in front of the glowing portal, looking between the flickering pulsing energy field and each other.

"You sure you wanna go first?" Bronn asked. He was up on his feet again. The juice that Jonson had given him miraculously accelerated the healing of his wound so that it was just a scar now. He would limp for a while, but even that would go away over the course of a few days. He was standing just a few feet behind me, a wooden crutch under one shoulder and the handgun that I had given him in the other hand.

I nodded and looked round at the others. "Everyone ready?" I asked.

Some nodded, some looked nervous, and a few said nothing. Of course, they were as ready as they could be. Though they'd been anticipating this moment for the best part of a decade, when it came down to it, and even though life was difficult in Riverfall, none of us really knew what we would find on the other side. I had shown them the book that JH wrote, and sat and read the description of the lands on the other side and of JH's encounter with the very first group of exiles that had gone through, and of course Ellis, but much could have changed in that time. We were still heading into the unknown.

I nodded to Ilya, and we stepped through together into darkness. I immediately raised my weapon and moved forward, trying to focus through the lack of light. I'd found a headband with a working torch attached to it amongst the Stygian supplies, and it came in handy now. I switched it on and it cast a beam of sharp light across the floor. Ilya helped with the lack of light the moment she appeared next to me, somehow delayed by about five seconds. The area was illuminated even more brightly as her strange glow filled it.

This wasn't what I had expected. This wasn't ruins in yet

another city, as JH had encountered when he stepped through. No, we had appeared inside some form of building. Not thirty yards away, I could see the nearest wall. Dotted here and there, built in a grid, were columns made of bricks, holding up a roof that was maybe forty feet above us. The spot where I appeared was clear – a large open space inside a building maybe hundred feet across. Most of the walls were built from either scrap metal or a strange mixture of masonry that must have been salvaged from many different buildings.

My eyes began to focus, and I noticed small peep holes in the sides of the building, all at about shoulder height. It was then that three of the exiles stepped through behind me, all with raised weapons, and then another followed, pulling the first of the trolleys. I moved out of the way, further into the building, and stood next to one of the columns, scanning the room and the walls for an exit.

One of the exiles looked worried. "I don't know," I said. "Just stay calm and stick to the plan. We'll get out of here." They nodded, and we waited for the others to come through. When everyone had arrived, Jonson did a headcount, nodding, looking at every face, making sure no one had been left behind.

One by one, more of the exiles switched on torches and lamps, and the light cast across the room intensified.

I noticed that light was shining through the peepholes, bright almost enough that it could be day outside.

"I'm going to take a closer look," I said.

"Careful, now," said Bronn. I looked at him and nodded before starting to move toward one of the peep holes in the wall nearest to me, checking the ground as I went. Ilya followed me, staying close. The floor didn't look trapped in any way – there were no raised spots, or slits that could hide a collapsing section. It just looked like tarmac, like you would see on a road.

"This is the place," I said, sure of it. "Someone built this around the arrival spot."

Bronn heard me and nodded, looking a little more relieved. The exiles were still bunched near the arrival clearing, but they had spread out a little, aiming weapons in all directions.

I reached the wall but stopped a few feet away. I leaned forward to look through the small peep. The light was bright, and it took a moment for my eyes to focus on what was beyond. It was daylight, all right, not synthetic. I moved my head to the side to see further round and spotted a small perch below the peephole, like something a weapon could be leaned on.

Outside I could see the street, or at least part of it. Ruined buildings surrounded the area, but a little further along the street, a large wall loomed, also built from various scrap materials.

I stepped back, frowned, and then moved directly across

to the other side of the room and peered through another hole. More tumbledown houses greeted me, but beyond them the same wall.

"This whole place was built to contain whoever arrives," I said. "This is a way to stop those coming through from escaping."

We were in a trap, I thought, but I didn't voice that. The last thing we needed was panic.

"Why would they do that?" asked Bronn.

"Maybe the Stygians used the portal sometimes." I looked around at the walls. There were burn marks all over.

"There's a door here," Bronn said. He moved away from the rest of the exiles. "Looks barred from the outside."

"I'm going through," said Ilya.

I nodded. "Be careful."

Just before she stepped through the wall, we heard voices outside. I called for her to stop, but Ilya was gone, stepping through the metal barrier to the other side. The room darkened a little.

The voices continued to talk, but I couldn't make out the words. I had a guess that one of them spotted Ilya as she stepped through the wall, because the speaker's tone changed from calm to panicked. Then an alarm sounded – a long wailing siren that grew in intensity.

"Dammit," I said, looking around. We needed to get out of the trap, but judging from the burn marks on the walls, I didn't think blasting our way out was a quick option.

"Get into one corner," shouted Bronn. "Out of the centre." Everyone obeyed, rushing to one of the corners, and pulling some of the smaller trolleys with them to use as cover. I hurried over and joined them, crouching behind one of the trolleys and aiming my gun over the top. If there was going to be a fight, we weren't going out quietly.

Then I heard Ilya's voice speaking, slowly and calmly, though loudly. Her words were muffled by the walls. There was an answer, shouting at first but then calming to speaking level. The sound of many boots on the tarmac outside preceded guns starting to appear, pointing through the peepholes.

Then came a different voice, also muffled but sounding calm, not as panicked as the first. A minute ticked by and no one fired. It was quiet outside but for the sound of Ilya and the newcomer's voice.

Then the voice called out. "Bronn, is that really you in there?"

Bronn croaked and coughed. "Yes," he shouted. "It's us."

"It's really you?" asked the voice again. "Get the lighting up. I wanna see them."

There was a series of clicks, and some strip lighting in the ceiling flickered to life, illuminating the huge room much more brightly. A hatch opened, high on the roof at the far end. For a moment, it was empty, and then a large sheet of clear glass was raised in front of the gap, and a face appeared. It was a man, maybe in his forties. I didn't recognise him, but he peered across at the group of us. Bronn straightened up and moved forward, out of the crowd of people.

"Oh God, it's them!" shouted the man. "Get those damn doors open. Put your guns away. Get them out of there!"

Then doors opened around the room and daylight flooded in.

"Are any of you hurt?" the man called, still watching from above.

"Just me," said Bronn. "But I'm good." He started to hobble over to the nearest door.

Armoured figures stepped into the building, weapons lowered, looking all around, checking the corners. "Any Stygians?" asked one of them.

"None," I said.

The man frowned at me and then turned and looked away. "Should we be expecting any?"

"Not for a while, but it's possible," said Jonson. "We finally managed to take their fort, briefly, thanks to this young man and his ghost friend's help, but they could be back to reinforce the place at any time."

"Do they come through here much?" asked Bronn.

The man shook his head. "Not for a long time. It's probably two or three years since they last sent some through. That's what we built this for. Early on, they came through. We thought that you'd make it sooner, but we couldn't come back and help. Of course, when the attacks started coming, we guessed you were trapped or lost. We would have come back for you if we could have."

"I know," said Bronn. "I know you would have." He frowned at the man. "Is that Rod?"

"Yeah," said the man. "It's been more than ten years."

Bronn struggled toward the man, who lowered his weapon before stepping forward and hugging him. "This is my nephew, Rod," he said. He shook his head. "It's been so long. How are your father and mother? They make it through okay?"

He man nodded. "Yes, yes. Father's not so great these days. He's suffering with his joints, and still from some of the wounds he got when we made it through, but he's ok otherwise. Ma is doing fine. You know, not many were lost at all in the battle. We raised the place. We expected you to follow. After all this time, most thought you must have all died, but we still hoped."

"Only my other brother, your uncle Jono, fell on that day," said Bronn. "We've lost a few in the years after, but most are still alive."

I looked around, watching as these people were re-united with people they knew. The younger ones, at least, were now all smiling and then it occurred to me. They'd all been children when they'd been stranded back there with just a few adults. These young men and women, now all in their late teens, some even in their early twenties, had lost contact with their parents ten years ago. One of the exiles walked by carrying Henry the cat, who wriggled upon seeing Ilya, jumping out of the exile's hands to run over to her.

"And who are you?" asked Rod. "I don't recognise you."

"Connor," I said, holding out a hand. "Connor Halldon."

He didn't take my hand, instead his face went pale. "Connor Halldon? *The* Connor Halldon?"

"I don't know any others," I said.

"Is your mother Eleanor?" he asked.

"Yes, the very same," I said. "Apparently she was your leader for a while and helped you get through? Has she moved on, now? She must have been gone for years." I presumed that much, at least; that after she helped the exiles through the portal, she would have gone on and continued her search for her parents.

"No. She never left," he said. "She's…" his voice trailed off as he looked over my shoulder.

"Connor?" asked a voice behind me.

I froze and slowly turned.

There she was, after all these years. My mother. She looked almost the same as she had when I last saw her, all those years back, as she sent me off to school. Maybe there were a few creases around her eyes, but other than that, she was the same.

Then we were holding each other tight.

I'd finally found her.

:: Record Date 16:07:4787 21:53

So I'm recording this while sitting in my own room in the settlement the exiles have built from the ruins of the Ashlands town.

The last few hours have been a complete blur, a mixture of sadness and extreme happiness. More of the latter, I'm glad to say. Not only was I with my mother, but I also discovered so much more.

She had ended her journey to follow JH, and to find her parents, because of things that had happened in the years that she had been leader of the exiles, but I'll get to that in a moment.

There aren't just a few exiles. There's hundreds and hundreds of them, probably even a thousand, all living in the town and the surrounding area. They've taken over most of the town and even rebuilt some of it. Apparently you can even watch a film in the cinema that JH camped in when he was here, though they mostly use it as a theatre because they really do only have one film.

Over the years they've cleared the area completely of any of the horde remnants like Shamblers, and they've even built a wall around most of the town, blocking the outside and the Ashlands out.

It's impressive, and it kinda reminds me of Evac City, in some ways.

After many tears, and my mother apologising again and again and again for not being able to come back for me, she took me to the base and introduced me to a man called Evans – her husband and now my stepfather. He's a tall man, with broad shoulders and a big, bushy beard, and he towers over me. Quite imposing, really, until you get talking to him. It wasn't long before we were sharing some of his home-brewed beer and laughing on the porch of their house.

Later on in the day, I found myself standing before two little girls, maybe seven years old.

Mina and Yara. My sisters.

This was why my mother never left. She got as far as Riverfall, met Evans, helped the exiles escape to the Ashlands, and then didn't go any further. She'd had a choice, you see – one that was impossible to make. Go on in search of her family or stay with the one that she knew was still alive.

No choice at all, if you ask me.

I could see how torn between the two options my mother still was, even after all these years, but the choice seems to have come down to those she knew were alive and those she was unsure of. She found love and then became pregnant, and when the two girls were born, there was no choice anymore.

"I stopped hearing GreyFoot when you were born," she said. "I don't know why that happened. I thought maybe something had gone wrong and the poor thing had finally passed away to wherever the Maw go when they die. I had no clue as to whether she was even still there, and I had a family here. I'd spent time with these people, and I realised that one day you might come, you might find the trail that I'd left behind.

"So, my journey ended, and I never did carry on. It was difficult to accept, but between the girls and Evans, and the possibility that you might find me again, I decided that the fate of those that were gone was no longer in my hands. I knew I couldn't go back to you without being caught and arrested, and probably getting you into trouble in the process, but I've never stopped thinking about you. Of course, I never stopped thinking about my parents and grandparents, either.

"I have searched for portals," she continued. "I hoped to find one that led back to Gaia, but I never found one. I had no way to return. I could only hope that you'd lead a good life, or that one day you'd find me again.

"I thought of carrying on many times, and I even started making plans, putting equipment together several times, but then I think of the girls and Evans, and you, and I stop. I know there may be more at stake than the lives of my family here, but I can't do it. I can't be responsible for that, now."

It took a while for me to get my mother to open up and tell me all of her journey. At first, she seemed reluctant to talk about JH, my great-grandmother, and of course her parents, and it was even more difficult for her to talk about what else she had abandoned by staying with the exiles. There were still secrets untold. The mystery of JH's disappearance, and the final fate of Nua'lath and the others, remained unanswered.

This leaves me with a quandary, now. Do I stay here, as my mother did, and help build this place? Or do I go on?

One last thing happened before I went to bed. There was another call from the portal trap, and the siren went off again, but then stopped. I went to see what was going on – where I'm staying is only a few streets away from there – and found none other than Allon, the man from the wall, had come through. It took me awhile to explain his presence to the guard, but eventually they let him pass. It turned out that now the exiles were no longer in the city, he was no longer bound to his vow to stay.

I've no idea what he has planned but I'm somehow glad he isn't stuck up on that wall on his own anymore.

:: Record Date 17:10:4782 09:00

It's over three months since I arrived at Ashdale – that's what they decided to call the place – and although I have a place of my own now, out near the farms on the edge of the town, I'm still itching to finish the journey that my mother couldn't. She argues against it, every time I bring the subject up, but the last time we spoke, she was more resigned, if maybe a little sad. She even said she'd speak to the council and see if they could put some equipment together for me.

It seems that if I do go, I'll be making the journey alone, and I think that's what worries my mother the most. Ilya was keen to carry on when we first arrived, but I think that was because she hadn't found her calling. Now that's changed.

Over the last two months she's been teaching at the school. There are over a hundred kids there, including my little sisters, and from the moment Ilya started teaching them – after they got used to her appearance and weren't afraid of her anymore – she must have fallen in love with all of them. She also has her own place, right near the school, and of course Henry the cat moved in with her. He never gave her any choice in that.

Now, after two months, she seems to have settled, and she doesn't talk about moving on, anymore. When I last spoke to her, a week ago, she finally shook her head and said she had too much to leave behind, now.

So my preparations stalled for a while, but over the weeks I began putting together the kit I'd need. I've been making extra trips out into the wilderness to hunt. There aren't many creatures here, but there are some strange badger-like things. They're vicious animals that tend to damage what meagre crop farms the exiles have managed to plant on the outskirts of the town. A lot of the land further out is just grey ash, burnt and lifeless – nothing grows there – but some areas near the town are still green. I guess that's what draws the creatures that live in this place towards the town in the first place.

Anyway, the badger things are big, but one shot is still enough to take one down, and they cook up ok. The meat dries into a very hard and chewy texture, and with enough added salt – something in abundance further out from the town – and wrapped properly, once it's dried out thoroughly, it works as a decent field ration. Should last a long time, as well. I have bread biscuits, of course, the staple of the town, which are made from wheat grown out in the crop fields and cooked into a hard flatbread, but I don't want to take too many of those. The exiles need all the food they can get, and it's their biggest problem, most of th[e time?] I have been putting aside some whenever I've bee[n] any, but I'm not about to delve into their supplies.

I started modifying the assault rifle, and oh it's awesome. I must admit, it's possibly even better than my old one. Amongst all the junk that they've gathered in the town supply, I found a scope that wouldn't work for any other weapon. I think it's from an older model of shredder rifle, and they don't have any. I managed to modify it to fit mine.

I've kept some of the batteries we brought from the haul in the Stygian fort, thinking that I kinda deserved a few of those as long as I didn't take too many. There were a lot of them – hundreds, in fact. I've stashed a few as backups for my guns, though I now only have the rifle and one handgun. The rest of the stuff I gathered I've handed over to the exiles. I'm pretty sure I don't need that many guns.

I've got armour made from ex-Stygian gear and some badger-thing skins. The technology the Stygians used was stolen from the Resistance, and pretty close to the same thing, enough so that the batteries work with a little modification. My mother figured out a lot of this from the ones that they managed to take when they made their escape years ago. Just a quick modification and all the batteries that we took on our raid were reusable, not just with the Stygian equipment but with the old Resistance equipment as well. I've found a large portable lamp that can run on one of the batteries and illuminate a huge area – no being in the dark for me.

Lastly, I salvaged an old sleeping bag, added extra

pouches to my old rucksack so I don't have to carry two of them, and I also fixed a very small but fast working water still that drawers draws moisture from the air and kicks out a little drip or so every minute. It's not super-fast, but if I left it running it would fill a bottle in maybe four or five hours.

I should be okay.

:: Record Date 18:10:4782 15:12

I found myself, after just over three months, standing by the portal at the petrol station where Nua'lath slaughtered many of his kin, or so JH had said.

The Ashdale folk have long since cleared the area of corpses and have built a small outpost there to keep an eye on the portal.

Another one-way portal. I'm hoping that I'll be able to find a way back.

"You seem reluctant to go," Ilya said. Now that I was there at the portal, preparing to say goodbye to a mother that I'd only spent three months with after not seeing her for well over a decade, Ilya was right.

My mother was sitting on a chair a few yards away, her eyes a little red. I could tell she was trying to keep her composure, but she had been crying before.

"Are you sure this is what you want to do?" she asked.

No, I wanted to say.

"Somebody has to," I said. She was about to reply, maybe offer an excuse and another apology as to why she didn't carry on, but I cut her short. "I didn't start this journey to not find out, and as much as I really want to stay, we still need answers."

My mother looked embarrassed.

"I didn't mean it like that," I said. "Your circumstances are different. I don't have young children to watch over."

"I know," she said. "I just wish it could have been me that could have gone, but I've got too much here, now. I'd hoped that you could be part of that."

"I will, when I've found them and brought them back," I replied.

She smiled. "So optimistic," she said.

"There has to be some hope that they're still alive, or if not, then maybe I'll find where their final resting place is and at least we will have an end to it."

"It's bothered me so much, for all these years, with no answer," she said.

"What about after?" asked Ilya. "What then?"

"I know the route back here," I said. "If I have to go the same way through The Corridor again, through Riverfall, then that's what I have to do. Even if the Stygians retake the fort, I can sneak through. If I've got JH and the others with me then we can all get through. I'm sure. Somehow, I'll find my way back here. And if I can get hold of one of those keys, like JH had, or if he still has one, then we can use it to come back. "

I'd come out to the portal at the petrol station to look at the markings on the floor many times. I'd spent hours staring at them, memorising the shape – every turn and twist in the pattern – so it was now burned into my memory. I wouldn't forget it, and it would be my way back if everything else failed. I'd just need one of those keys and the knowledge to use it.

"Do you have everything you need?" my mother asked, standing up and giving me one last hug.

"Yes," I said. "More than enough, really. I may have to ditch some, it's so heavy." I turned to Ilya to say goodbye.

"I wish you weren't going alone," said Ilya. "I'd come, but, you know. The children need a teacher."

"You don't need to apologise," I said. "You've found your place here. You belong here. And I wouldn't want to risk any of the others going with me."

"I'd send everybody with you, a whole army if I could make it so, but no one wants to leave," said my mother.

"No. I don't blame them, now they have this place," I said. It was too much. I had to go before I folded and gave up. I would only be back here again in a few weeks, putting them through this all over again.

"When I have my answers, maybe I can come back. I promise I'll try," I said, stepping toward the portal.

"Don't just make it a maybe," said Ilya. "Be here. Good luck."

I nodded. My mother held her hand out, and I grasped it one last time, squeezing tightly, before I let go of her hand. I turned and stepped through the portal.

I was surrounded for a moment by a mesmerising glow that fizzled, even in the bright desert sunlight. The power emanating from the thing was incomprehensible. I wondered for a moment whether it could be harnessed in some way. Imagine the power that could be generated.

I was plunged into darkness, but that only lasted a second before I flicked my headlamp on. I was so glad I found that before we left the Stygian fort. The box in the warehouse had been full of them, and I never did hand it back. I lifted my newly modified assault rifle and peered around me, checking the floor for obstacles.

I had to move quickly for this part.

I had spent many hours going through it with Ilya, my mother, and Evans, pouring over JH's diary and the notes my mother had made. We roughly figured out his path from the hall of spiders, and I had even staged a mock up in one of the empty town buildings, just so I could get this part right. A delay here would kill me.

I turned left. The darkness receded away from the glow of my headlamp. It has about a forty-foot range that lit up ahead of me brightly and dimmed at about thirty feet. The place was exactly as JH had described it. Scarily so. How it could remain almost unchanged over the years was eerie.

A vast hall of brick – even the ground was made of brick – with crumbling columns and a stairway that only led up about twenty feet before it ended where it had collapsed. That way I would ignore. I would also ignore the massive cobwebs in the corners, and I put aside thoughts of the shuffling sounds around me as the creatures awoke from their slumber. I didn't have very long.

I started jogging away from the dais, taking the few steps as quickly and quietly as I could, then started across the open ground until I saw the archway. A shriek came from the darkness behind me, far across the hall. I ignored that too, and seeing the archway drove me on. I increased my speed, running on toward the entrance of the tunnel that would lead me away from the things that lived in that place.

There was no telling how many of the creatures there were; all that mattered was that they were still here, after all this time. I could hear the movement around me, the shuffling and clatter of legs on stone. Another shriek sounded, but it was further away as I passed the archway and hurried into the corridor.

Now, I sprinted. I had been working myself up to this for a while, spending many hours running, jogging, building up my fitness level, ready to make my escape from this hall. It was, I knew, the one key point in JH's journey, after entering The Ways, that would be of greatest threat to me. Some of the creatures further into this strange realm may also be dangerous, but to be caught in the spider hall would be a very swift end.

Thankfully, after about ten minutes of running, I saw another archway ahead of me. The spiders hadn't followed JH as far as another hall. I slowed to a stop and took out the note paper from my pocket, quickly re-reading the next instruction.

I would pass through this and several other halls before I reached the one I would climb out of. Hopefully that would lead me up into the hall of pillars, that vast and endless space above.

:: Record Date 18:10:4782 20:15

Found a crevice in the wall of one of the passageways between the halls. It was just big enough for me to crawl into. Beyond the opening was a small collapsed section of brick that give me enough room to sit down and lean against the rubble. I piled up some of the bricks in the entrance until there was only a very small gap. Of course, if something knew I was in there, it wouldn't stop it, but hopefully I'd wake before they managed to get to me.

I'm exhausted, having run almost non-stop for the best

part of a day. I need to sleep now, because the next hall I reach will hopefully be the one where I need to climb the steps up into the hall of pillars. That's if our estimates are correct. I've only a guess of just how long it took JH and the others to get up there.

:: Record Date 19:10:4782 07:32

Some interesting noises while I was asleep last night.

Something came by and sniffed at my temporary wall – yes, *sniffed*. Not a spider, unless these ones have grown noses.

I waited a good hour until the thing moved away, then I gathered my things, kicked away my wall and peered outside with my headlamp switched on. No traces of anything along the corridor in either direction, so I carried on, hurrying this time. I wanted to be away from the area. I'm sure I could deal with most things with the weapons I've got, but I'd rather avoid a fight if I can.

This place is creeping me out enough without the thought of creatures sniffing around after me.

We were almost right in our guess that the next – and tenth – hall would be the one with the stairs, but it wasn't. I moved on, heading quickly through the passages to the next, and found what I was looking for.

I didn't bump into the sniffing creature, so I guess it must have gone another way. There are enough passages heading off the main one that it could have gone anywhere, really.

So, I made the stairs about two hours after setting off. The hall was much the same as the others, vast and cold with a roof of endless blackness. The stairs seemed undamaged, and I could see them winding round and round the outer wall, up into the darkness above.

I was glad I'd camped out and rested, because they go a long way up.

One big, deep breath and I began the climb.

:: Record Date 19:10:4782 09:45

Just as JH described, some of the stairs had fallen away in places, and I'm pretty sure I just climbed over the gap that he described jumping over. I'd read this part of his diary over and over, and I knew that a section of the stairs fell away, so I was prepared for a climb, but it wasn't too bad. Even though the stairs had fallen away, making the gap too far to jump, there was still a ledge about a foot wide sticking out from the wall. I expected it to fall away at any moment, but it didn't.

More stairs. I'd been at it for about two hours, so I had no idea how far I'd come, but it was getting a little dizzying, going around the stairs. JH had said he climbed these stairs for three hours, but I'm beginning to think that was a bad estimate.

I decided I'd sit down and eat before trying to go further. It's so quiet here; there's barely a sound to be heard. That's probably why I heard the scratching noise below.

I shined my beam down the stairs, past the gap, and saw something dark scuttle away, back down the stairs. Whatever it is, it's not a spider. It's the size of a person on all fours, and furry. I didn't catch any other details.

So, it seems I do have something following me, at least this far. Maybe it won't be able to get across the gap. I thought of firing a volley down the stairs, but I decided against it. I don't want to draw more attention to myself from other creatures that may be wandering around down here.

Time to move on.

:: Record Date 19:10:4782 12:05

I finally made it to the top of the stairs after another hour or so – JH's estimate was probably better than I thought – and collapsed in a heap. I'd never climbed so many stairs in my life and, having considered it now, I think maybe I should have added stair-stepping to my fitness regime. Too late now.

My thighs were numb, as were my feet. I decided to sit at the top of the stairs for a bit and let my body recover. Also, this part was the critical bit of the plan. I needed to go in the right direction or I could be lost in this place forever.

I sat eating some more badger jerky, looking out across the open space. The plain stretched ahead in all directions with very little difference and hardly any features breaking the monotony.

JH had mentioned moss that glowed, and I could see a glimmer of light in several directions. It was an eerie glow but there was little for it to light up – only the open ground.

My mother and I had discussed this part of my journey, and we couldn't come up with a solution. The best that we'd ended up with was Ilya saying I'd think of something when I got there, but then my mother mentioned the dead Stygians.

JH found one of them not far from the top of the stairs and followed a scattering of corpses for a while before he met Sha'ris, but we all agreed that there could be little left after all this time. There was a chance, though, I thought, and I stood up, still chewing the dried meat. I scanned the flat ground, slowly turning in a full circle, until, after doing that three times, I spotted something that may not have been rubble. It was, as JH had said, about a hundred yards away. There were fallen bits of rock everywhere, but this didn't look like rock, and it was nestled in a patch of the weird moss.

I unpacked my portable lamp, deciding that in this big open space I needed more light than the headlamp. I picked up my gear and started out across the open ground, lamp in one hand, rifle in the other.

I reached the edge of the moss, and frowned, unsure whether I should walk on it or not. I decided to tempt it. Nothing happened when I stepped on the moss. There were no big explosions, or flashes of light; no bursts of deadly spores were released to kill me. There was just a soft crunch under my feet.

I was right. It was a pile of bones. I moved closer, some dread thought entering my mind that the thing would spring to life and attack me. You never know, do you? With all the other odd creatures I've seen or heard about, a living skeleton wouldn't surprise me much. I stood a few feet away from the remains, peering at them, making out the shape of the bones and finally the curve of the skull. That was all that remained. It was humanoid but different enough that I could tell it was a Stygian.

I'd found the first breadcrumb of my trail.

If this one was here, then the chances were that there should be more not far away. I scanned the flat horizon and spotted them straight away this time – distant piles of remains – and I headed quickly over to them. I came across another half dozen skeletons further on from that, scattered across a long line leading into the darkness between the patches of glowing moss.

Then, further on, I found a circle of bodies around a

small space maybe ten yards across. I stood in the centre, holding one arm out, judging the distance. Yes, this would be where Sha'ris had stood, surrounded by his dead kin. Surrounded by the ones he had killed.

Now I knew I was heading in the right direction, except this was the last of the bodies. I had to find the other markers that would follow, and all that lay ahead was open ground. JH had discussed the great pillars, and that lay ahead somewhere, but they had walked for a while first.

I stood looking at the open plain ahead, stuck, unsure where to go, and it was then that the sound hit me.

The noise had been there for a while before I recognised it. It hadn't drawn my attention enough, I guess. I'd been so intent on following the trail of the dead, and just thinking about everything that had happened, when the noise finally filtered through.

It started very quietly, but as I listened I managed to concentrate on the low sound, it became clearer. A groaning noise, like straining wood. It was a deep sound, and every time I heard it I felt a brush of cold wind blow past me.

The tree. It had to be. The groaning. All I had to do was find the source.

I walked across the open ground, treading around smaller patches of moss as I went, heading in what I thought was the direction of the groaning sound. Occasionally I'd skirt around a hole that seemed to go down into nothingness, an endless drop, and the thought of falling in sent a shiver up my spine, so I chose to keep my distance from them after looking down the first one.

I walked across open ground for a good half an hour, hoping that I was keeping a straight bearing in the right direction. I stopped a few times, convinced that I was wrong, but then I thought otherwise. The sounds *were* getting louder, the further I went.

But the endless plain just went on and on, until... There, in the distant darkness, was a shape. Was it a pillar? Had I reached the hall of pillars? A large bulk stuck up from the ground – a darker silhouette against the blackness. I moved quicker, jogging now.

Hell. It wasn't a column at all.

Just as I got within fifty feet of the thing, it shifted and leaned towards me, revealing its true nature and size.

The description that JH wrote in his diary doesn't do this thing justice – unless it's grown since then. I suppose it could have, but I also think that the thing was ancient enough that it was vast a long time ago.

Standing there at the foot of the tree, looking up at boughs that must be fifty feet thick, I wondered how such a thing could come to be. It grows out of the ground, breaking through the bricks. There are piles of them stacked up around the bottom, along with even more debris, which seems to be evidence that the tree grows right up into the vaulted ceiling, hundreds of feet above me. There's no foliage on the tree, just bare trunk, but the bark has things living on it – or *in* it – creatures the size of my fist crawling across the surface and burrowing into cracks.

When the thing swayed, there were glimpses of some kind of light, way, way up in the canopy, but I wouldn't dare trying to climb up the thing. I don't know what those bugs are, but they look like they could bite a good chunk out of someone. Wouldn't want to get caught by a mass of them.

I walked around the tree. The trunk must be a hundred feet or more in diameter. I kept my distance, but even that was difficult. Long, trailing lengths of vine dangled down from the branches, and I didn't know if it was just my paranoia, but they seemed to be reaching out for me. They never touched, and only got within a few inches of me, seeming to hover around the area, avoiding contact.

Was this some strange way in which the tree could feel its way? Was this thing aware of me? The idea that such a monstrously large thing could be sentient in some way scared the absolute crap out of me. I really hoped the thing couldn't walk. No. That was a crazy idea. I mean, walking trees? Sentient, walking trees? No.

What if it trod on me?

I didn't stick around to find out. I was sure that some of the bug creatures were crawling away from the tree, getting closer, maybe testing me, so I headed off into the darkness beyond.

I needed to find somewhere else to hide for the night. Hmm, of course there wasn't really night here, was there? It's pretty much all night and no day. But I would still need somewhere to rest. So, I pressed on, not wanting to be near the tree or any of those things when I settled down to sleep.

:: Record Date 19:10:4782 15:34

I'd only gone another hundred yards when I saw the first row of pillars.

I'd been wondering what they would be like. The section of the book that details this part of JH's journey is very rushed, with little to no description. I guess he was recovering from the battle when he finally filled in those bits, and he must have been quite weak.

Anyway, I knew that as soon as I found the tree, I would hopefully find the hall of pillars, and the holes in the ground, and maybe – just maybe – the tank. The chances of running across the exact spot were quite unlikely, I know, but the lit area of this place seems to follow a set path. I did wander further outside it but found that the unnatural light dissipates after a few hundred yards, and I ended up in near pitch black around the beam of my lamp. I quickly panicked and ran back to the area of ambient light.

Even though it's dim, the ambient light is enough to see

a good distance by. The lamp is bright, but only for maybe thirty or forty feet, and from there I'm dependant on other sources. With those bugs wandering around, and God only knows what else, the thought of being in the dark scares the utter crap out of me.

The pillars were massive, about forty feet wide and made from the same ancient bricks that the ground is, and they rise endlessly into the darkness above me. The light that allows me to see seems to drop off at about three hundred feet, and unlike in some areas, like where the big tree was, the ceiling isn't visible. They are spaced about two hundred yards apart.

I headed to the nearest one and found a hollow section of wall inside one of the pillars that goes quite deep – deep enough to hide in. There are also large holes in the ground. I walked over to one of the holes and shone my lamp down it. I looked away when my stomach churned.

There was no end to the drop, and the best way to describe it would be to imagine the ground having been melted away. The very edges of the pit are still made from the same materials, but it's almost like the bricks have been melted. The chasm itself seems to be sheer, with no holes, cracks or other details.

Puzzled, I moved away and headed back to the hole in the pillar to make camp. I wouldn't be able to block myself in, like I had down in the passages, so I started to crawl into the alcove until a section of the wall next to me cracked and started to fall away. I hurried out of the hole and watched, panicked, wondering if the entire column would collapse, but all that came out was a spew of dust.

Yeah. I decided to find a different camp and switched on my lamp again, heading further into the hall of pillars, keeping what I thought was a straight line as I passed from one to the next.

The moss seems to grow in patches where water drips from above. I have a good supply of water in a couple of plastic bottles, but I haven't had the chance to use the distiller yet. That would require a semi-permanent camp. But it's good to know that there is water here; at least I know I should be able to gather some if I need it.

Four columns further into the darkness and I settled next to an intact one with a pile of rubble around it. I was hoping to find my next marker – the tank – sooner, but going further would have to wait. Hell, it wasn't like moving fast would make up for any of the last few decades. I didn't need to hurry too much, yet.

:: Record Date 19:10:4782 19:28

I drifted off for a while, maybe twenty minutes, but awoke to a noise nearby. I'm damn lucky that I was hiding next to the rubble, because if I'd been in the open ground I think I might be dead now.

The creature sitting just a hundred feet away was massive. Easily thirty feet long. I remember the descriptions of the giant slug things, the gargants, that JH mentioned in his diaries, but this was not one of them.

No way.

This thing looked a little like a rhino – or at least it looked similar to the pictures I'd seen.

Or a dinosaur.

Except there was a row of spikes across the top of its head. Its body appeared to be covered in a dark, rough exoskeleton of some kind, so it couldn't really be a rhino. Also, I think it was probably much bigger than they are.

I sat there, as quietly as I could, not wanting to draw attention to myself, and just watched, wondering what the hell I was going to do. I couldn't guarantee finding somewhere safe to bed down every time if things like that were wandering around, but that wasn't the current concern. How the hell could I get away from this thing without being noticed and squashed?

Then I saw them, rushing through the darkness.

I knew Kre'esh, and had killed a few that I'd encountered, but I'd never seen a hunting pack.

And they were heading straight for my hiding place.

The creatures were fast, but I got a bead on one of the Kre'esh as they sped toward me, when the Rhinospike sniffed and launched into action.

Adrenaline charged, I was about to fire, thinking the first Kre'esh was in range, but the Rhinospike charged towards them, flailing its head and moving into my line of sight. Two of the Kre'esh broke off from the pack and circled back around the huge monstrosity, seeming to attempt to draw the thing away, but it ignored them, moving much faster than I'd expected as it swung its massive spiked tail, catching the leading two Kre'esh off guard and smashing into them, sending them flying into the darkness. I'd never seen anything like it. One moment the Kre'esh were there, and the next they were barrelling through the air, flying hundreds of feet away to crash, dead, to the ground.

The other two Kre'esh backed away from Rhinospike as the behemoth snorted and flailed.

Then something strange happened.

The two Kre'esh backed away and started heading around the creature, like they planned to make a long detour to avoid the thing, but the Rhinospike just shifted its position, watching them move back and forth.

Each time the Kre'esh tried a different route the Rhinospike put itself between them and me.

The Rhinospike bellowed a long, deep noise that reverberated through the ground, then sniffed and swung its tail again, threatening the Kre'esh.

Was the creature protecting me? That was an odd

thought.

Then the rubble pile twenty feet away moved, nearly making me jump out of my skin. The rocks fell away and the creature that had been hiding underneath climbed out of the hole.

It was a smaller Rhinospike.

I was sitting in a damn nest.

I waited, unmoving, to see who would make the next move. I was ready.

Then they were running, splitting apart and taking a different route toward me – and the baby Rhinospike. The mother was forced to strike at just one, and caught it with a swing of her tail, smashing into the ground with a loud, echoing thump that sent a shock wave rippling through the ground.

But the second Kre'esh bolted towards the younger Rhinospike, completely unaware, it seemed, that I was there.

I opened fire, sending a volley of shots toward it, hitting it on its side and sending it to the ground, reeling.

Then I was off, grabbing my rucksack and running for it. As I expected, Mrs Rhinospike was not very grateful to me for saving her child, and she seemed far more interested in tearing me apart as she had the Kre'esh.

As I ran across the hard ground as fast as I could, I thought for a moment that she would just keep coming and

I'd be dead, but at a hundred yards distance from the nest, she slowed and turned back.

I just kept on going. I was not stopping.

I jogged on, my lamp showing the way across the open ground, as I headed towards what looked like another of the huge columns. Except, as I got nearer I started to notice differences. This column wasn't the same. Up at about thirty feet high was a ledge built from wood, and a long rope ladder hung down to the ground.

Who the hell builds a den in a place like this? I'd no idea, but it was a welcome sight. I needed to reach somewhere safe to rest.

As I climbed up to the ledge I saw something move in the darkness. I stopped, grabbing my gun and turning my headlamp to where the movement was, but whatever it was scuttled away quicker than I could see it. I saw what I thought might be tentacles, but it could be something else.

I do know that the thing was as big as me.

I hope tentacle thing can't climb.

:: Record Date 19:10:4782 21:40

So, my final bed for the evening was about thirty feet up from the ground, on a ledge made from wood, built by God knows who. I'm not questioning it, though. Not now. I have enough puzzles swirling around my head for now that the origins of a little wooden ledge are minor. At least I'm able to sleep. If I were down on the ground again I think I'd just sit there.

Nope. Tentacle things can't climb up here.

There are four of them on the ground below me, looking up. If you can call it looking.

I think those are eyes looking at me, but I can't be sure. They're kinda bulbous and black, with no iris, so it's hard to tell. I can't even tell how many eyes the things have.

:: Record Date 20:10:4782 04:41

The tentacle things have gone.

I woke up having not slept well. I'm having weird dreams.

I thought I was asleep up on the ledge, but I found myself moving quickly along the ground below. Or was I crawling? The tentacle things were everywhere, but as I moved closer to them they moved away, slithering back into the darkness. I could feel my heart thudding as I ran among the things. There were other figures moving alongside me, dark shapes that I couldn't recognise.

But then, the weirdest thing. I looked up and saw the very ledge that I was sleeping on. How could that be? How was I down on the ground looking up at myself?

Then I woke and sighed. It had been a dream. I moved to the edge of my platform and looked over, right down at where I had been dreaming that I was.

There was nothing there.

I'm going to try and get more sleep.

:: Record Date 20:10:4782 09:27

I had another strange dream. It's almost as though the second I get off to sleep the weirdness begins. I was crawling on the ground again, or whatever I was doing. Somehow, I seemed closer to the floor. This time I was moving away from the pillar, but I did glance back and could still clearly see the ledge in the distance.

Then I was breathing heavily, moving swiftly through the darkness at a speed that I knew I wasn't capable of. Still there were many others around me, but I didn't know who they were, only that I belonged, somehow, with them. I wasn't carrying any gear in the dream, so had nothing to slow me down. After what seemed ages running through the darkness, and passing other pillars, I skirted around more of the holes, and then jumped up high, landing on something dark and heavy. Metallic.

I looked down and saw that I was sitting upon a large vehicle of some kind.

Then I was sitting up, sweating, and nearly falling off my

ledge.

The tank. It had to be.

I don't know if the dream was right, and honestly, I don't know how I'm sleepwalking without actually going anywhere, but if the dream is true then I'm not far from it, and therefore I'm not far from the chasm. A couple of hours, I think the diary suggested. Just a couple of hours away.

:: Record Date 20:10:4782 11:09

And, damn it, the dream was right.

I climbed down off the ledge, nearly falling at the bottom of the rope ladder before I got my bearings and started out. It was eerie, seeing some of the things that I saw during the dream appear before me, but it was also useful as a judge of the direction. I remembered turning at some point in the dream and heading out in another direction, so I had to keep a careful eye out for the signs.

The first was a pile of rubble, smack in the middle of a patch of the strange moss. Which reminds me – I stopped yesterday to get a closer look. There was something blurry about its appearance and my curiosity went into overdrive.

The stuff moves.

Creepy.

It actually sways backwards and forwards. To what purpose, I have no idea. I guess it's something I may never find an answer to.

After about half a mile I found the second marker from the dream – a trio of holes in the ground. They are much the same as the others I've passed, just huge dark chasms with no apparent end to the drop. The only difference was that these three were so close to each other.

I edged around the holes and turned, roughly changing my direction to what I'd seen in the dream. I would know soon enough, I hoped. In the dream I passed through a massive field of moss, and there was a path running directly through it.

Two hundred yards away I found the moss field. It was much bigger than it had appeared to be in the dream, stretching out into the distance in all directions apart from the one I had come from.

No path, though. Odd.

I turned right and walked along the edge of the field, but after a while I started to think I'd gone the wrong way and I turned back.

I found it after about fifteen minutes of walking, which makes me wonder if I was recalling the dream correctly. I must have misjudged the distance. But, then, it *was* a dream.

Eventually the field ended, and there it was, smack in the middle of the open ground between two huge pillars. An ancient tank. Or at least the remains of one.

The tank.

The rusted heap looked as though it had been sitting there for centuries, and so did the bodies scattered around it.

I climbed up onto the top of the tank and sat on the crumbling and jagged remains of the turret. The gun was still in place, held on by rust alone, I think. Most of the outer panelling of the vehicle had rusted away, and I could see piles of mangled metal dotted around the area.

I was close, now. Close to where I needed to be. I sat there in the darkness, looking out across the expanse of brick ground ahead.

I grabbed my rucksack, took out JH's diary, and flipped to the section that he wrote about this part of the journey. If I'm reading correctly, the distance could be as little as a few hundred yards. There are mentions of dark slithering things – maybe that's my tentacle things?

The section describing this part of the journey is extremely brief, barely a few paragraphs.

Grabbing my gun, I jumped down from the tank and headed in the direction of the string of dead remains that littered the ground. There were half a dozen of them, and they appeared to have been picked clean of all flesh. Now, only bones and rags remained.

And I could see nothing in the distance.

The diary mentions bright light and booming noise, but I'm presuming that was caused by the portal Nua'lath had been opening at the time. There's nothing but the darker darkness now. The sort away from the patches of moss.

:: Record Date 20:10:4782 14:34

I walked maybe three hundred yards, jumping at every sound and movement in the darkness. And there was a lot of movement. Dark tentacles slithered and snapped at me only twenty feet away, and I felt the air move near my face as a hissing resounded close to me. I turned, raising my gun, and only just managed to fire at the thing, causing it to screech and shy away, backing off into the darkness.

They don't seem to like the lamplight, but it also doesn't deter them too much. The ambient light that has been present for most of the journey seems to have gone, or it just doesn't exist in this area. I don't know.

I moved slowly, unsure of where I was going, spinning on my heels and firing into darkness when the tentacle creatures came too near me.

Then I fell.

I thought for one dread moment that I had dropped into one of the big holes, and I was going to just keep falling, but less than a second passed, just long enough for my mind to catch up and my heart to jump, and I called out. The cry was stifled as I hit solid ground and the wind was pushed from my lungs.

The lamp hit the ground and blinked out.

My head spun. I'd landed on something just a few feet down the drop. I felt around me and found the lamp, thinking, as the darkness seemed to rush in, that my main source of light had been broken, but it had just switched itself off when it hit the ground. I flicked the on switch and it leapt to life again, illuminating the area.

I had fallen onto a winding stairway that wound its way around yet another chasm. I pointed my light down into the darkness below and saw rock pillars, debris, burned ground, and other things littered around the bottom of the pit.

The throbbing in my head increased, and for moment my vision blurred.

Surely not a phase? Not here?

I looked up. Nothing, though in the distance, far away, I heard a screech, which sounded like one of the tentacle creatures, and then silence once more.

I started down the stairs.

This could be it. This was it. This had to be the place I had been searching for. How I had managed it confounded me. To actually find my way here?

I reached the bottom of the pit and walked into the

middle. It was difficult to see all of it. The lamplight didn't cast quite enough light to reveal the whole area, but one by one I spotted details scattered across the floor.

Scorched ground. Chains. Some rope.

A headless body that was long dead and dried out.

No head anywhere to be seen.

There were signs of a campfire just near the bottom of the stone dais – small, broken bricks placed in a circle to surround the charred remains of the fire. Next to it was a small pile of broken pieces of wood.

I knelt down, grabbed the wood, and put it into the campfire, dropping my rucksack and searching for anything I could make a fire from.

The only paper I had was the diaries, and I would never burn them, but I found a box of firelighters in the bottom of my pack.

One flick of the flint at the top of the firelighter and the thing flared. I dropped it into the dry wood and seconds later the flames began to flicker.

And the chasm around me was lit up.

And the tentacle creatures, hundreds of them, backed away and slithered back up the walls away from me.

There was no way I could fight them all. There were too many. I would have to grab some of the spare bits of wood, of which there were only three pieces, make torches and somehow get out of this place. The creatures don't like the fire light or the lamp, so hopefully they will back off when I try to leave.

And that gave me all of two seconds to try and figure out what I'd found.

I looked around, trying to find, but most of it was just as it was in the diary, as it had been at the end. I even found a patch of very dried blood on the ground and a spent injector nearby. JH had lain there.

Damn.

Then I spotted the bag on the ground and scrambled for it, pulling open the flap and rummaging inside.

A flare! And more firelighters.

I searched further and found three more ration packs stuffed into the bottom of the sack. But there was nothing else.

I glanced at the deeper chasm on the far side of the pit and then over to the chains lying on the ground near the centre. Had they been the ones that Nua'lath had used to chain his four icons? His gate openers? I couldn't see collars at the ends.

Puzzled, I walked over to the deeper chasm and glanced down into the darkness. There was, as I'd expected, no apparent end to it. Where it led, I've no clue. But I did guess that this was the pit that GreyFoot had fallen into.

I grabbed my rucksack and pulled out the contents, digging to the bottom to find what my mother had given me. It was stuffed right in the bottom – as small bag that was heavy.

Then I got to work.

It was the net she had made when she was younger. A pile of thin lines – most probably high-quality military lines, and a large, thin sheet – fell into my lap.

:: Record Date 20:10:4782 17:09

I've set it up after a bit of messing about. There are four lines, each long enough that the net, when lowered, disappeared into the darkness below. I'm not sure if that's a good thing or not.

My mother had spent a lot of time working on this, I thought as I secured each of the ends of the draw lines. Each had a pair of clips attached to it, with separate offshoots of line so that it could be attached to almost anything. This was a bonus for me, and I found a decent, broken bit of heavy brickwork to wrap the cord around for three of the lines, but the last was barely attached inside a hole that was a little too close to the pit, but it was all that I could find to secure that end onto. I hoped it would be enough to hold the net should GreyFoot fall into it.

Now all I could do was wait.

I've never been able to talk to the Maw, or at least I've never had the opportunity, having never met one, so I've no way to let her know I'm here, or that the net was set up, waiting for her.

I paced the area for a while, glancing every few seconds at the chasm, and finally decided I needed to get on with other things. Somehow, I need to find a trail to follow, whether GreyFoot could be saved or not. And so far, I've nothing to give me a direction of travel.

JH moved out of here at some point, along with Adler, Rudy, and hopefully my great grandmother and my grandparents, but where to? Did they manage to open another portal and go through? Unlikely, since they didn't have a key after Sha'ris took JH's.

So, they must have gone somewhere else.

But where?

I needed a clue.

:: Record Date 20:10:4782 18:43

The slithering creatures don't like the blue moss.

I discovered that purely by accident while exploring above the chasm. After searching around the bottom of the pit for a while, and finding little to help me figure out where

JH and the others had gone, I decided to broaden my search and headed up the steps.

Hundreds of the tentacle things followed me at a distance as I made my way out of the chasm and around the edge to the opposite side, where there is a massive patch of moss stretching as far as I can see. I noticed that the tentacle things stopped a few feet away from the stuff.

It got me thinking. I could make a temporary camp inside the mossy area and leave some stuff there. No. I'd have to go back to the ledge to sleep, because there were other things around that may not be bothered by the strange plant, but at least I would have a place to go to avoid the tentacle things.

And it was as I stood there in the moss, contemplating setting up a camp there, that I spotted it – the one thing I really hadn't expected to find in there.

At first, I thought it must be a large chunk of rock that had fallen from high up, but as I stood there, peering through the haze, I realised that the shape was much too angular and very recognisable. It was also further away than I'd thought, and therefore much larger than it first appeared.

It was an APV – an armoured vehicle just like one of the ones parked in the vehicle depot back in the bunker. How it had got here, I have no idea, but I rushed over, weapon drawn, wondering if there was someone else down here.

The side doors were wide open, and the inside of the

vehicle was covered with rust and grime. All eight of the wheels were deflated and the panel glass that covered the front driver's bay was smashed. Piles of thick glass were scattered across the ground outside and all over the inside of the cab.

No electrics. I tried to start it, but the motor didn't even turn over.

So, no new vehicle, just a rusted old thing long abandoned. But, more importantly, there were signs that the vehicle had been used as a camp, and from the rubbish gathered in one corner, and scattered outside, it had been for quite a while. There were no supplies, not that I expected to find any, but there was a bag of empty plastic bottles that could be used to store water. I may set up the still and start stockpiling.

The front of the APV is completely caved in, as though it had crashed, or came in contact with an angry Rhinospike?

:: Record Date 20:10:4782 21:07

I managed to push the side door shut and wedge it there. It's damn heavy, but the runners were still working, and after I cleared some of the grime off them with a rag that I found, the door slid open and shut easily enough.

Normally these doors would be shut magnetically, but the power running the vehicle was long dead. The catch at the top of the door works, though, so I can lock myself in.

The driver's compartment at the front is open to the outside, but there's a solid barrier and a small door between the main compartment and that, so with both doors shut I'm pretty much sealed in.

Going to settle down to sleep. I made a bed in one corner, rustled up from rags that I found strewn around. It's not comfortable, and it smells pretty bad, but it's much better than the cold, hard stone or the uneven wood up on the ledge.

Progress. Even if only a little.

I no longer need to go back to the ledge, and hopefully that will mean I won't draw the tentacle things out of their nests anymore, and I'm much closer to the pit.

There must be more clues here, somewhere. The APV being here is unexpected, and the only thing I can think of is that it was there before. Did JH use this as a camp or someone else?

After I've slept I'll examine the outside and see if there is something that I've missed. But right now, I'm just glad to be sleeping inside something made of metal rather than on a cold ledge high above a mass of things that seem to want to eat me.

:: Record Date 21:10:4782 04:12

There was movement outside during the night. I woke to the sounds of scratching at the front of the APV and scrambled to grab my guns. There was no way in unless whatever it was could smash its way through metal plating.

I looked out through a split in one of the panels and saw something large and dark move past – certainly not GreyFoot sized – but couldn't make out any details. What I did hear was sniffing.

I'm pretty sure the tentacle things didn't have noses.

Something else is out there.

Great.

:: Record Date 21:10:4782 11:43

I slept for hours! And I was hungry when I woke, so I wolfed down some badger jerky.

Then I went outside and searched around the area where I'd heard the sniffing, mainly to see if there was a way into the vehicle that I hadn't noticed. I'm not sure how I'd patch something up if I found one; maybe I could just block it up with rubble or trash.

I didn't notice it at first, but it must have been watching me the whole time. I turned around, looking out into the darkness back towards the pit, and saw something move in the corner of my vision. Initially I thought it might just be another chunk of rubble, but then it moved again.

I spun round, raising my gun and taking aim, but then I stopped.

All I saw was the pile of rubble.

I edged forward slowly, rifle raised and the sights trained on the pile. It looked as though something had broken through the ground at some point. Bricks were scattered in a pile surrounding a hole about a foot wide.

I frowned and shone my headlamp down into the hole, noticing what appeared to be the entrance to a very thin tunnel carved into the ground. I hadn't really considered what the surface would be like underneath the layer of bricks, but this gave me my answer – tightly packed gravel and stones.

The entrance looked well-used and worn smooth, as though whatever had created it travelled this way frequently, but the tunnel curved away after dropping about three feet. I couldn't see any further into the strange warren. I looked across the open ground in all directions and saw that there were several other similar piles, though they were all at least thirty yards apart. Something moved in the darkness below at the very edge of the light.

It couldn't be the creature that I'd glimpsed the night before; that had been too big to fit in the tunnel. This was something smaller.

I headed back to the APV.

:: Record Date 22:10:4782 13:18

A trip back to the chasm told me that nothing had changed. My net was still rigged up and the cords weren't taught, so GreyFoot can't be in the net. I wish I had some way to communicate with her, to tell her that the net is ready to catch her, but I don't, and even if my mother had come with me, she lost the ability to speak to GreyFoot years ago.

Too many puzzles. Too many things I need to figure out.

:: Record Date 23:10:4782 11:26

I finally got to see the creature from the warrens.

I was sitting on top of the APV, eating some jerky, when I spotted the thing scuttling across the ground, far in the distance. It's a rodent of some sort, not unlike a rat, though somewhat larger. I don't think it's much of a threat to me – at least not on its own. It doesn't seem didn't seem that interested in the APV. I guess the vehicle has been part of its environment for quite a while now, maybe all its life. It's possible it smelled me and just came to investigate. Maybe it was its shadow I saw, that night, and that made it seem bigger.

When I move a light, such as the lamp, or move about

too much with my headlamp on, it scuttles back to its hole. I did try pointing the headlamp at it to get a better look, and it froze for a moment before belting across the floor to hide in the hole. I didn't do it again. The thing doesn't seem dangerous, unless there are a lot of them, and I don't want to torment it.

:: Record Date 23:10:4782 16:12

A few hours later I was sitting on the APV after making another trip back down the chasm. I'd taken a short walk out into an area of pillars I'd not investigated, when I noticed something leaning against the pillar over near the rat holes. I'm surprised I hadn't seen it before. The area is covered with moss and quite well lit, but there you go.

Sitting against the column, among a pile of rubble, was a body. I walked slowly across to it, weapon raised – just in case some of the tentacle things showed up – and stopped a few feet away from the remains.

It was a Resistance Vigilant, or at least what was left of one. Had I found the mysteriously missing driver to my APV? That was possible. JH certainly didn't mention an APV in the diary.

I moved closer. Whoever it was had been dead for a very long time, long enough that a dusty, white skull looked back at me through the visor. A few feet away a handgun – another shredder – had been dropped, and the figure's hand rested next to it. In the centre of the chest was a gaping blast hole.

Out of curiosity, I did check the body, but found nothing of interest, apart from the fact that it was wearing a full suit of ablative armour that, even if old, was in good condition if you ignored the hole in the chest plate.

I spent an hour or so burying the body under a pile of rubble, leaving the chest plate and visor on the top as a marker of sorts. I stood there afterwards, thinking I should say something but nothing came to mind. In the end I just nodded, picked up my salvaged armour parts, and left.

:: Record Date 24:10:4782 10:19

The armour was in near mint condition once I cleaned it up. Some of it is quite bulky, so I stripped it down and threw aside some of the bigger parts until I had arm, leg groin and shoulder guards.

Nice.

I feel a little guilty, but the previous owner isn't going to be needing it anymore.

:: Record Date 25:10:4782 06:15

I woke with a start and tried to stand up but was hit with a wave of dizziness and nearly fell over again. I gripped the side the wall the APV and closed my eyes, waiting for the nausea to pass. When it finally receded, I slumped back down onto my makeshift bed.

Damn it. I hadn't left the dizziness behind me in Riverfall, after all. Unless this was something different. It didn't *feel* different. The only odd thing was that nothing in my surroundings changed. I hadn't phased to some other version of this place. Maybe there were no other versions?

I'd felt nothing in the Ashlands for the whole three months I'd been there, and now this was the second dizzy spell since I arrived in The Ways.

Rather than get back off to sleep, I decided to take a walk outside, just to clear my head. I grabbed my gun but left my rucksack on the floor. I wasn't planning on going very far. I grabbed the lamp as I opened the door and headed out, unconsciously walking across the moss towards the stairwell that led down into the chasm. I was awake, so I figured I may as well go down there and check the trap.

Then I stopped. No. Too far. I turned and headed toward the rat holes. Maybe my new neighbours would be busy at this time. I'd only ever seen one or two around at any time, but I was always concerned that there might be more in those tunnels.

As I started toward the nearest mound, I noticed something lying not far from it. I stopped.

It was one of the rat things, but this one wasn't moving,

and it was most definitely dead. From what little remained, I guessed that it and had been chewed upon by something very hungry.

I spun around but saw nothing, no movement in any direction. Something was out here – something big enough to chew on a rat thing.

A Rhinospike? A Kre'esh? I didn't know. I suspected if a Rhinospike was around I'd have heard it, but either way, it wasn't safe out in the open anymore. I hurried back to the APV and was barely thirty yards away when there was a flash of movement on the roof of the vehicle.

Something large leapt up onto the top and stood there, over the entrance, watching me. I went to raise my rifle but only got it halfway up when another flash of nausea hit me.

Damn bad timing!

I nearly dropped the gun staggered, but then, as quickly as the dizziness had arrived, it was gone. My ears popped.

"You took your time," said a voice.

I stood still, staring at the beast upon the top of the vehicle, then glanced around. The thing looking down at me was much larger than any dog or wolf, maybe twice the size of the biggest dog I'd ever seen, and it was much more muscular and lithe. Its fur was a light grey, and a row of sharp spikes, or spines, stuck out along its back.

A Maw? It certainly fitted the description, but the Maw

had vanished during the war with the Stygians, after JH disappeared, and had rarely been seen since.

Large, bright eyes peered at me as it bared its teeth.

"Don't like to speak, then?" said the voice.

I took a few steps back, frowning.

"Oh, dummy," said the voice. "In your head, not your ears. When are you people going to get used that one?"

"You're talking to me," I said.

"Yes, in your head, not out loud," replied the voice.

"But, and I'm not…"

"No, you're not the James man. Come on. Get there quicker," said the voice.

"Yet you can talk to me."

"Yes! We're nearly there. Your mother was Eleanor, and your great, great, great something was the James man, and that makes you Connor, and I've been waiting as very, very, very long time. I thought your mother was going to come and fix my problem, but her thoughts vanished way back, and yours took their place. Your baby babble and your strange human young thoughts… Total nonsense, most of it."

"I can hear you," I said, still unable to grasp what was happening. I was a descendant of JH, but that didn't mean I automatically had his skills, did it? I thought it was a learned thing, not something that could be inherited.

"You can!" said the voice. "Maybe you can listen now, too. Oh boy. I'd hoped the babble was gone, but we're going to have some work to do, aren't we?"

"You're GreyFoot!" I said.

"Yes! Got there! That didn't take too long, did it?" said the voice.

:: Record Date 25:10:4782 08:41

"As I was saying. I was waiting for a long time, you know," said GreyFoot. "Not that I want you to feel guilty or anything, but you took your time. Couldn't you have maybe started a bit sooner? Quite boring just waiting around. And your mother was supposed to be here, not you."

She was walking alongside me, now, as we headed through the darkness. I glanced back towards the APV a couple of times until it disappeared from view. I was going to miss the protection of sleeping inside the thing, but GreyFoot was impatient and wanted to get going. I guess she was eager after so many years trapped.

"Yes," I said. "Well, things changed for her. Me, for example."

"Really," said GreyFoot. "I had to wait because *she* changed? How inconvenient I am. You turning up wasn't part of the plan. She was supposed to come and get me out. Not have a baby and lose her head and all that. Have you any idea what it's like, listening to a baby chatter to you constantly? I couldn't shut you up."

"Sorry about that," I said. "I didn't know anyone was listening."

"Babble, babble, babble, and then suddenly nothing. Nothing at all for all the time in the universe, until I started getting flashes of what I thought were memories. I thought I was going bonkers, but then I realised it was you. You were in that place with the big walls."

"Riverfall," I said.

"Yeah, maybe. Never been good with names. I don't know what triggered it. Maybe you went somewhere that I'd been or remembered something."

"I was in The Corridor before that," I said.

"I don't know what that means," said GreyFoot.

"The dark place that you were in with JH – the James man – before you went to the place with the big walls," I said.

"Oh, there," replied GreyFoot. "Yes. Not a good place. I liked the dark but not the smells and the things."

We walked on through the darkness, passing more of the columns until it opened out onto another vast, flat plane. I stopped at the last column, and GreyFoot walked on for a few steps before turning back.

"Where are we going?" I asked.

"They left me a trail," said GreyFoot. "DogThing did. A trail to follow."

"Like a scent?" I asked. "You can still sense it after all this time?"

"Not a smell. It's in the phase," GreyFoot answered, shifting impatiently and glancing over her shoulder into the darkness ahead. "I'm not sure how to describe it. I don't know if humans really understand the phase."

"No," I replied. "I certainly don't, though I think I might have used it a little by accident. So where does this trail lead?" I started to walk again, feeling exposed out in the open away from the pillar. Not that they would offer much protection. There were patches of moss, but only small clumps dotted around. It seemed drier; I couldn't see anywhere where water was dripping from above.

I was glad that I set up the still. For the few days that I had been at the APV, the little box clicked away, gathering moisture from the air, and I collected some water in bottles. The still has a neat little nozzle you can pour dirty water in and it gradually filters it. I now had half a dozen full bottles.

"This way," said GreyFoot.

"That's it?" I said with a smile. "No details, just a direction?"

"Yes," said GreyFoot. "Just a way to go. Where DogThing went, and all the others. Your people, as well. This is where the James man went, following that dark fellow."

I stopped again. "The dark fellow?"

"Yes, what's his name?" The dark one that's tall and quite grumpy."

"Sha'ris?" I asked, though I wouldn't have described him as grumpy. Maybe stoic.

"Sort of, but no," said GreyFoot.

"You're not making a lot of sense."

"The one that the James man has been fighting," said GreyFoot.

"You mean Nua'lath? He's dead."

"Not really," said GreyFoot.

My jaw must have bounced off the ground. "What do you mean?"

"You ask that a lot."

"Well, explain then. Nua'lath was killed. Cut in half by the portal closing. He's gone."

"I know," said GreyFoot. "I was there. He was chopped into bits by the glowing door, then he became the other one."

"Other one? Nua'lath died. It says it in the book. He was destroyed. Sha'ris took his heart." I dropped my rucksack, opened it, and rummaged around until I found the book, opened it to the last pages to read it to GreyFoot, but then I remembered. The last pages weren't in the book anymore. The last section was where they found the tree.

Dammit. I knew those missing pages would be important.

"I can't find the bit I need, but I remember it from the books in school. Sha'ris cut out his heart, brought back JH's family from the portal door, and then left."

"Nope," said GreyFoot.

"What?"

"That's not what happened."

"Then what did?" I couldn't understand. But there was a nagging thought tugging at the edge of my mind now. Why were the pages missing in the original book? I flicked to the back again and looked at the spine.

It was there all along and I just didn't see it.

There were no missing pages. What I had in front of me was the end of the journal. JH never wrote about after the battle.

"What happened after the battle?"

GreyFoot sniffed and started walking again. I quickly

bundled everything back in the rucksack, grabbed my gun and caught up with her.

"The other one that was like the dark man…"

"Sha'ris?" I said.

"Yes. He brought the bits of the dark one back, and then he cut out his heart."

"And?"

"And ate it. Then he started acting strange. He got angry and beat up the James man even more. I tried to bite him, and I got a good grip on his ankle, but he kicked me away and I fell into the pit and had to phase before I died. You see, the one you called Nua'lath took over the one called…Sharas? So, he didn't die, even though he had. A bit like when we phase, I suppose. We can almost die and still come back. He sort of did that, but to another body."

"And then what?"

"Then I didn't know anything until DogThing and the others phased back. The James man was on his own, still healing, but with his ghost friends. The dark one, in his new body, was gone. He'd run off. This way. So, they waited until James man was better and followed him. I don't know why he just beat him up but didn't kill him."

"You're saying Sha'ris became Nua'lath." This thought made me shiver. "And he never brought JH's family back?"

"Yes. He couldn't. The portal was closed," said

GreyFoot.

"And he couldn't open it again? His power was drained," I said.

"Yes," said GreyFoot

"Which means…all those years ago, JH and Nua'lath were still stuck in here. They were stuck in The Ways."

"Yes," said GreyFoot. "Which is why we have to follow the trail and catch them up. I think we're quite a long way behind them."

"Thirty years or more," I said.

"What's that?"

"We're probably thirty years behind them," I said, staring out into the darkness. The Ways was supposedly endless. They could be anywhere. "So why didn't they help you?"

"They thought I was dead," said GreyFoot.

"Oh," I said.

"I was young, still little, and didn't have the strength to speak to anyone. I couldn't tell them I was alive. I couldn't speak to anyone from the phase until I was older."

"You spoke to my mother."

"That was after a long time stuck in there. I'd grown. I don't know how I was able to speak to her. I shouldn't have been able to. She was on a different world."

We walked on, the ground still completely flat in all directions. If I hadn't had GreyFoot with me, I would have no idea where I was or which direction I was going in.

"Do you think you can find them?" I asked after a while.

"Yes," said GreyFoot. "I can just follow the trail to DogThing. Come on, we've got quite a bit catching up to do."

"If we ever manage to. I could walk for thirty years and not find them."

"Don't be so grumpy," said GreyFoot. "You want to try waiting all that time in the phase with nothing to do. This is much better. This will be fun."

WHERE NO RIVER FALLS

About the Author

GLYNN JAMES, born in Wellingborough, England in 1972, is an author of dark sci-fi novels. In addition to co-authoring the bestselling ARISEN books he is the author of the bestselling DIARY OF THE DISPLACED series.

More info on his writing and projects can be found at

Website - www.glynnjames.co.uk

Facebook - www.facebook.com/glynnjamesfiction

Goodreads - www.goodreads.com/GlynnJames

WHERE NO RIVER FALLS

Printed in Poland
by Amazon Fulfillment
Poland Sp. z o.o., Wrocław